THE RIGHTEOUS ROAD

BCC PRESS

BY COMMON CONSENT PRESS is a non-profit publisher dedicated to producing affordable, high-quality books that help define and shape the Latter-day Saint experience. BCC Press publishes books that address all aspects of Mormon life. Our mission includes finding manuscripts that will contribute to the lives of thoughtful Latter-day Saints, mentoring authors and nurturing projects to completion, and distributing important books to the Mormon audience at the lowest possible cost.

The stories in *The Righteous Road* show off Ryan Shemaker's impressive range, from the dramatic to the satiric—he is a writer who can make you feel deeply in one story and laugh aloud in the next, a rare gift.

—T.C. Boyle
Author of *The Tortilla Curtain* and *Blue Skies*

Shoemaker is one of my favorite short story writers, and this book exemplifies all that makes that statement true. He hooked me with the interplay of LDS culture, our scriptural underpinnings, and our foibles and peculiarities, handled with nuance, fantastic writing, and style. I relished every single story. There was not a miss in the entire collection. Some of the stories left me laughing out loud. Another left me pondering for days the way we deceive ourselves about our own motivations and actions. But all of them captured me with their excellence and fun. Don't miss this collection. It is a treasure trove of meaning and delight.

—Steven Peck
Author of *Heike's Void* and *A Short Stay in Hell*

Family, faith, loss, love and hope—these are the essential elements of Ryan Shoemaker's beautiful stories. A troubled, reckless father, Kurt Cobain, Adam and Eve—Shoemaker weaves gritty reality with the myths of our most ancient stories illuminated by a contemporary imagination that is sure-footed, honest, and unflinching—all while infusing his sentences with the kind of understated humor that you have to earn by living with an open, compassionate heart. Bravo.

—Jason Brown
Author of *Why the Devil Chose New England for His Work: Stories* and *Character Witness: A Memoir*

THE RIGHTEOUS ROAD

STORIES BY
RYAN SHOEMAKER

The Righteous Road: Stories
Copyright © 2025 Ryan Shoemaker

For information contact
By Common Consent Press
972 East Burnham Lane
Draper, Utah 84020

Cover design: D Christian Harrison
Book design: Andrew Heiss

www.bccpress.org
ISBN-13: 978-1-961471-26-9

Printed in the United States of America!

10 9 8 7 6 5 4 3 2 1

For Craig and Gaylyn Shoemaker,
who always gave me their best.

For Jen, who's always in my heart.

For Joe, my fellow traveler.

Contents

Acknowledgements

The stories in this collection were first published elsewhere:

"Come as You Are" in *New Ohio Review* and *Made in L.A. Vol. 5*; "Light Departure" (as "The Cat's Paw") in *Santa Monica Review*; "Light Departure" and "The Private Investigator" in *Dialogue: A Journal of Mormon Thought*; "In That Classroom" in *Weber: The Contemporary West*; "The Water Between Us" in *Barzakh Magazine*; "The Righteous Road" in *Silk Road Review*; "Adam and Lilith. And Eve" and "The Lord's Sacred Funds" (as "Jesus (Almost) Visits the Mormons") in *Sunstone*; "Parley Young: One Mormon Life" in *Gulf Stream Magazine*; "Barry Dudson: The God Journals" in *The Path and the Gate*.

It is always difficult to explain yourself
to the faithful.

      —Kate Northrop, "Gardening"

If only we could feel safe and dare show each
other tenderness. If only we had some truth to
believe in. If only we could believe.

      —Ingmar Bergman, *Winter Light*

But as I raved and grew more fierce and wild
At every word,
Me thought I heard one calling, *Child!*
And I replied, *My Lord.*

      —George Herbert, "The Collar"

Come as You Are

"Bruises on the fruit, tender age in bloom."

—Kurt Cobain, "In Bloom"

"He walked out the back door of Exodus and climbed the six-foot wall . . . over the next two days, there were scattered sightings of Kurt."

—Charles R. Cross,
Heavier Than Heaven:
A Biography of Kurt Cobain

Thursday, March 31, 1994, my eighteenth birthday. That was the day Scotty and I helped Kurt Cobain out of a tight spot and then jammed with him in my basement. I know what you're thinking—I'd have thought the same if it hadn't happened to me. But it did. This was back when I played guitar and Scotty drummed, back when we had this crazy idea, like a million other kids drunk on the grunge zeitgeist, that all we needed to be rock stars were some ratty jeans, a thrift-store cardigan, three guitar chords, and enough repressed angst to pen the next great teenage anthem. But that was years ago, six days before Kurt put a shotgun in his mouth, before Scotty really did become a rock star, and before I stopped caring about all of it. That day I met Kurt, that changed everything.

▪■■▪

It happened like this. There we were at Tower Records on Sunset Strip, Scotty and me, free from Burbank for a couple hours. Soundgarden's "Spoonman" pounded through the sound system, Chris Cornell's raw-edged screech lifting our spirits as much as any Mormon hymn we'd sing at church on Sunday. And all those albums spread out before us!

My fingers flew through the CDs. Alice in Chains. The Melvins. Mudhoney. Nirvana. Pearl Jam. "Someday," I whispered to Scotty, "our album will be right here."

Scotty took a breath that could have sucked all the air out of Tower Records. "Yeah," he said. "Right here. Our album."

And then we heard this slurred voice rise above Chris Cornell's vocal blast. A wasted butt rocker, a relic from another era, in a denim jacket and tight, acid-washed jeans, was ragging Shaun, the cashier, about the music.

"Man, all you play now is this grunge shit," the guy griped. "What happened to Mötley Crüe, man? What happened to White Snake and Twisted Sister?"

"What happened?" Shaun said, throwing us a wink. "They're all in rehab, dude. They're all fat. They're done. Look for the reunion tour at the county fair."

Scotty and I laughed at that, what a lame-o, all while sneaking a glance at the cute hippie girl down the aisle from us in a black Pearl Jam T-shirt and Birkenstocks. Golden hair parted down the middle, ten perfect toes painted a bright aquamarine.

Then this other girl showed up, a round blush on her cheekbones, panting as she said to Pearl Jam Girl: "Callie, listen. This guy who works here said he just saw Kurt Cobain. Swear to God. The guy said Kurt just left, like a second ago."

Pearl Jam Girl grabbed her friend's elbow, dropped the CD in her hand, and they both shot out the door onto Sunset Blvd, their heads twisting east and west. Then, maybe, I saw a mess of long, ratty blond hair float past the far window and round the corner of the building. The girls must have seen it, too, because they screamed and ran.

Scotty eyed the door, his dark eyebrows rising like they were on strings. "You think?" he said.

We'd heard the rumor that Kurt Cobain, at that very moment, was in a Los Angeles drug rehab.

I grabbed a Melvins album. On the cover, a couple of creepy cartoon kids smiled and fawned over a two headed puppy. Sure, I felt the itch, too, to rush from the store, to hunt the parking lot and alleys—because perhaps it was Kurt Cobain. Just to see him, just to bask in his rebel aura and get his autograph, would be the chance of a lifetime. But it seemed so desperate, so pathetic, so uncool. "No," I said. "There's no way it's him."

▪■■▪

Fifteen minutes later we were back in my Ford Taurus station wagon, my mom's old car, squinting at the blurred figure on the cover of Soundgarden's *Superunknown,* my newest purchase. The silver Casio on my left wrist chimed. We didn't want to leave. But my dad would be pissed if I wasn't home by six thirty. He'd promised pizza from Tony's Bella Vista and a Porto's mango cheesecake for my birthday.

I turned the key and then cranked up the A/C. The car's interior had a tropical humidity, with a hint of mildew from a pile of damp blankets in the back seat we'd thrown on the grass a couple weeks ago at Valhalla Memorial Cemetery. A goth girl from AP English, Kami Boswell, claimed that at midnight on a full moon the spirits of the dead roamed the cemetery. She swore that she'd seen her grandmother there. I didn't believe her, or hardly believed her, but I had to try.

"You smell that?" I asked Scotty, catching a whiff of cigarettes in the car. And then from the backseat, there was the rustle of fabric and a low thump against the passenger side door. I caught Scotty's eyes as I turned to look, an electric tingle blitzing across my neck. The scuffed toe of a black, low-cut Converse poked out from under a blanket, and one blue, blood-shot eye glared at me through a gap in the folds. I was ready to bolt from the car, my mind filled with dangerous characters.

But then Pearl Jam Girl appeared at the passenger door and pounded a fist against the window. She panted, her part crooked, a hundred loose hairs lit by the sun. Moist stains bloomed under her armpits.

A muffled voice leaked from the blankets: "Don't tell them I'm here. Please." That voice! Unmistakable. A voice we'd heard a thousand times in MTV interviews, its cool, monotone bravado railing against the music establishment and sell-out bands, a voice that turned to gravel when screamed through a microphone.

Scotty cranked the window down. Pearl Jam Girl leaned in, her eyes wild, her breath coming in gasps. I could smell it, something like ammonia and saltine crackers. Her friend stood behind her, scanning the parking lot and bouncing up and down like she had to take a huge piss.

"Kurt Cobain," Pearl Jam Girl gulped. She had tears in her eyes. "He just ran by here. You see him?"

Scotty looked at me. For a second his eyes angled toward the pile of blankets. "No, didn't see anyone." He tipped his head until it touched the seat rest. "You see Kurt Cobain run by?" he asked me.

Pearl Jam Girl looked at me.

I tapped a finger against my chin, a casual gesture, an authentic gesture to suggest I knew nothing. "I wish—"

Pearl Jam Girl didn't stick around to let me finish the sentence. She and her friend were racing back through the parking lot toward Sunset Blvd, little wedgies from their jean shorts riding up their butts.

Scotty and I just stared through the windshield, not wanting to turn around, as if this whole crazy, unbelievable moment—Kurt Cobain hiding in the backseat of my car—might vanish. And then that voice again, pleading: "Get me out of here."

I shifted the car into drive and inched through the parking lot, stopping to wait for a break in the traffic on Sunset Blvd. Pearl Jam Girl and her friend were on the sidewalk, cheeks wet with tears. We could hear them through Scotty's open window, inconsolable as they gushed to four other girls, the contagion of mania. I recognized that hysteria. I'd seen it in the old black-and-white newsreels of rabid teenyboppers ready to tear John, Paul, George, and Ringo limb from limb. I felt a sudden righteous zeal, a clear-eyed vision: saving Kurt from them, carrying him to safety.

As we idled there, the traffic rushing past, the seconds ticking by, Kurt, in an explosive rush of air and movement, threw the blankets off. Scotty and I flinched. Kurt was at the window, rolling it down. The girls looked at him with dumb doe eyes and then with a recognition that settled in their jaws like a heavy weight, pulling their mouths open to show all those perfect teeth. They screamed, a deafening industrial shriek, bodies convulsing, fingers pressed to their faces.

"Hey," Kurt said, half his body out the window. That shut them up as they waited for him to say something. Instead, a low, fleshy sound churned in Kurt's throat. His lips and nose quivered for a half second. Then a spray of yellow mucus shot from his mouth and splattered the girls. Kurt flipped them two stiff middle fingers. "Pearl Jam sucks!" he yelled.

I stomped on the gas and squealed onto Sunset, hunched forward, hands knotted to the steering wheel. I didn't look back. I didn't want to see those girls' stunned faces.

Kurt took a huge breath, like a free diver surfacing from deep water. His forehead was slick with sweat. "Fucking parasites," he said.

I gave a casual shake of the head, like I agreed, though my heart smashed against my T-shirt so hard I thought Scotty might see it. "It's cool," I said, as if this were nothing; another day, another rock star saved from an adoring mob. But my thoughts were troubled by that image of Kurt, his sudden anger, his cruelty to those girls.

"No worries," Scotty said. A nervous vibrato rattled his voice.

Kurt laughed, a slow, easy chuckle that shattered the strangeness of the moment, a laugh dripping with sarcasm that eased my dark thoughts.

"I'm Toby," I said. "This is Scotty."

Scotty turned to look at Kurt. "We're in a band. I drum. Toby plays guitar. He's a lefty like you."

I cringed, as if Kurt Cobain cared about our band or that I was a lefty. We didn't even have a bassist.

"You play any shows yet?" Kurt asked.

The heavy traffic crawled along on Sunset Blvd. A woman in a black bra and lacy underwear, nine stories high, gazed seductively down at us from the side of a glass and steel apartment building.

"One." And then I hesitated to add: "Some high school battle of the bands thing."

Kurt leaned forward. He looked awful, worn out. There were dark crescents under his eyes and scabby red blotches on his forehead and cheeks. The watch on his wrist, the dial a man's grinning face, caught the sun and cast a point of white light onto the car's ceiling. Above the watch was a white plastic wristband, the kind hospitals give patients.

"Was it awesome?" he asked.

I shrugged. "We just played two songs. We only have two songs."

Kurt licked his dry lips. "But was it awesome?"

Our two songs were me screaming into the microphone and playing amped up, sped up, shorter versions of whatever I was learning in *Guitar World*. But there was something special about playing, if only for our friends in their ripped jeans and oversize plaid shirts, as Principal Thorton tried to break up the mosh pit. Up on stage, the strike of those chords, Scotty's steady beat—there was a rush of euphoria. "Yeah," I admitted, "it was awesome."

Kurt reached into his shirt pocket, pulled out a cigarette, and lit it. "Fuck yeah," he said, blowing smoke from the side of his mouth. "We once played in front of a grocery store, once in a RadioShack. Those were my favorite shows."

Smoke swirled through the car. Scotty and I looked at each other.

Kurt tapped the cigarette on the thin edge of the open window. "I need to get to North Hollywood."

·■·■·

We drove up Highland, past the Hollywood Bowl, and onto Barham. KROQ-FM oozed from the radio—the Gin Blossoms, Blind Melon, the Lemonheads—but the breezy silence sucked dry the music's electric cheer. Kurt sat there, hands crossed on his lap, a cigarette between his fingers.

"Shit," Kurt said suddenly, looking up at the Oakwood Apartments, a sprawling complex whose pitched rooflines seemed to hover over the tops of the thick trees edging Barham. "We used to live right there," he said, "that window on the corner. Dave and Krist and me. We recorded *Nevermind* just down the road." Kurt's lips curved into a pained grin. "There was this guy," Kurt said in a dry whisper that was almost lost in the rush of air through the open windows, "who lived a couple apartments down from us. Fucking annoying. Always knock ing on our door, wanting to hang out, never shutting up about this kids' show he did in the seventies and how his parents stole all his money, and then some new, bullshit TV deal he was working on that would make him millions. All day he'd wander the hallways looking for someone to talk to. We wouldn't answer the door. We hid in the bushes if we saw him coming." Kurt stared at his hands. Smoke leaked from his nose. "That kids' show he did, I'd wake up early every Saturday to watch it. But I never told him that."

Wind whipped through the car's open windows, bringing in the smell of eucalyptus and French fries and sewage. And then the San Fernando Valley opened before us, a brown haze pressing down on a tree-lined grid in full springtime bloom—a polluted Eden.

I couldn't believe the strangeness of all this, Scotty and me and Kurt Cobain. Yet Kurt was different; not the rock star from all the MTV interviews and music videos we salivated over. None of that aloof, anti-authoritarian hipness, none of the crazy antics with Krist and Dave, no hamming it up with fake French accents and silly faces.

"Fucking corporate radio," Kurt said, flicking his cigarette through the car window. "Why don't they ever play Mudhoney and the Melvins? And more fucking Nirvana."

"Yeah," Scotty said. "More fucking Stone Temple Pilots, too."

In all the years we'd known each other, I'd never heard Scotty swear.

Kurt glared at him. "You're shitting me, right? Stone Temple Pilots? They're fucking boilerplate commercial rock, Nirvana rip-offs."

Scotty wilted, his shoulders shrinking, his head bending forward.

Kurt picked at a purple scab on his chin. His hand shook. "I need a fucking phone," he said.

We were coming up on Burbank Blvd and Hollywood Way. I made a quick right into a 7-Eleven. Kurt had the door open before the car even stopped. He walked to a payphone and yanked the handset from the cradle.

Kurt shouted into the phone, his fisted right hand hammering the air like a tyrant making a speech. He stared down at the sidewalk, his back curved, his lips moving quickly.

I turned the radio down to catch a word or phrase.

Then Kurt dropped the handset, leaving it to dangle above the sidewalk. He slid into the back seat and grabbed a folded piece of paper from his shirt pocket. "Laurel Canyon Blvd and Saticoy. You know where that is?" he asked, squinting down at the paper.

"I think," I said.

I pulled onto Burbank Blvd and drove west. Beck's "Loser" played on the radio, that buzzing sitar and final blast of distorted guitar over the repeating chorus, and then a second of silence before the first ringing notes of Nirvana's "All Apologies" filled the car.

"Hey," Scotty said, pointing at the radio. "Nirva-na." He eyed Kurt like he'd pulled a rabbit from his ear. "How'd you do that?"

Kurt grinned. "When you're a big fucking rock star, you just make a call."

▪■▪■▪

I turned right on Laurel Canyon and drove north, the car suddenly rattling over potholes and seams of patched, uneven asphalt. We passed through the twilight of a graffitied underpass crowded with shopping carts and shadowed figures, the reek of piss wafting through the car. Scotty fidgeted in his seat, his upper lip coated with sweat. This was a world we'd only caught glimpses of from the I-5 and the 170, a blur passing at seventy miles an hour.

"Here," Kurt said, pointing to a gray, white-trimmed apartment complex at the dead-end of Saticoy. One side bordered the 170, and though I couldn't see the traffic, the sound of it was like the steady rush of the ocean.

Kurt opened the car door and stepped out onto a patch of dirt dotted with dandelions and crabgrass.

"We can wait," I said. "It's no problem."

"Cool," Kurt said, but he was fixed on the building, like he could see through the white cinder block.

He walked to a rusted metal gate and pressed a but-ton. Unable to stand still, those black Converse shuffled over the cracked sidewalk. The gate buzzed. Kurt pushed the door open, walked toward a dim hallway, and then vanished into darkness.

"You think it's true?" Scotty asked. "The drugs and all that?"

"That's the story," I said.

The hum of the freeway filled the car. Scotty stared at the spot where Kurt disappeared. "I thought he was in rehab."

"Maybe he was."

I thought of Rome. It'd been all over MTV for the last month: painkillers and champagne. Kurt in a coma. Some said Kurt was a junkie. Some said Rome was a suicide attempt. It made no sense. A rock star wife. A baby daughter. All that success. I didn't want to believe it. "What now?" I asked.

Scotty chewed his bottom lip, still looking at the dark hallway. "We take him to your house for dinner."

I laughed. "No way."

Scotty turned to me with a sly, crooked grin. "I'm serious. What a story we'll tell everyone on Monday."

"And my dad?" I said. "What would I say?"

Scotty had a look, something wild and hungry. "It'd be hilarious. Tell him that Kurt wants to be a Mormon."

I looked up at the building. Behind it, twilight filled the sky, a soft, luminous glow.

Several minutes later, the gate opened and crashed shut, and then Kurt was standing at the passenger window, drumming the roof of the car with his open palms, hips swaying, his silver wallet chain striking his belt buckle. He leaned into the car, his elbows resting on the open window. "Hey, rock stars."

I didn't know what to say. Scotty looked at me and then jerked his head in Kurt's direction.

"So," I said, tracing the raised Ford logo on the steering wheel, "it's my birthday today."

Kurt gave a euphoric smile. "Hey, man, happy birthday."

"My dad's getting a pizza," I said. "Just him, Scotty, and me. No biggie, but you want to come? Or not. We can take you wherever you want."

"Yeah, cool," Kurt said, with a smile that looked ready to slide from his face, and pupils that were black specks in the center of those blue eyes.

■■■

By the time we got to Burbank, crickets were trilling from every front lawn and under every bush. A few points of starlight leaked through the golden-blue light of Hollywood that illuminated the pale night sky. I was late.

"Didn't I say six thirty?" my dad asked as we stepped into the entryway. A Book of Mormon open on his lap, he sat on the living room couch, still in the beige Carhartt work shirt he wore as the manager of a small factory in Van Nuys that made bumpers for cars.

"This is Kurt," I said.

Kurt stood between me and Scotty, hands clasped together in front of him. I wondered if my dad recognized him, but I saw nothing of recognition on his face, only concern as he absorbed Kurt's stringy hair and torn jeans, this strange adult with his son.

"Hi," my dad said, a little cold around the edges. He closed the Book of Mormon. "Toby, can I talk to you in the kitchen?" Kurt's eyebrows shot up and his eyes went wide, one of those you're-busted faces. My stomach jerked. I had this awful image of my dad throwing Kurt out of the house.

We stood in the semidarkness of the kitchen, facing each other, the refrigerator humming, the microwave blinking the wrong time. My dad's thick arms crossed in a perfect knot over his broad chest. "Who's Kurt?"

I explained Tower Records and that Kurt was in this cool band and how he needed a ride, and because it was my birthday, I thought it would be nice to invite him over. And then I played Scotty's card: "And I think he wants to be a Mormon. Not that he came right out and said it, but maybe he's a little lost, like, spiritually." And I said it with a straight face, a gloomy note in my voice.

"Really?" My dad's head swung toward the lit entryway, where Kurt and Scotty stood. For the past six months, since my mom died, my dad had thrown himself into church, a newfound devotion, mumbling scriptures as he walked through the house, devouring thick religious texts by long-dead Mormon prophets. Now he was a ward missionary and greeter, grinning madly and shaking hands each Sunday at the chapel doors.

I felt bad about the deception, but then looking from the dark kitchen to where Kurt stood, at his pale blotchy face, I felt something unexpected claw my throat.

And then we were all at the table, a Tony's Bella Vista pizza box open between us.

My dad wiped his mouth with a napkin and then looked over at Kurt. "Kurt, Toby tells me you're in a band."

Kurt laid his half-eaten pizza slice on the paper plate in front of him. "Yes, sir." There was a formality in his voice, in his gestures, in the way he dabbed at the corners of his mouth with his napkin. "It's kind of a loud, high-energy rock band," he said. "I play guitar and sing. We're really hoping to make it big."

My dad leaned forward on his elbows. "And it's full time? It's your job?"

Scotty let out a little snort, then clamped his hand over his mouth. My dad looked at him, puzzled, and then back to Kurt.

Kurt stared thoughtfully at the pizza's wilted pepperoni. "Yeah, full time. Me and the guys. Nose to the grindstone and all that. We want to be famous. But if rock doesn't work, we'll try country. If not country, maybe reggae or opera or Inuit throat singing. And if that's a bust, I'll give up music for something stable, like being a sushi chef or maybe a garbage man or a logger."

"I see," my dad said, though I could tell he didn't know what to make of Kurt. Then: "Toby says you're interested in Mormonism."

Kurt looked at me, a narrow-eyed, I-got-this-dude look. Nine years between us, more than half my life, but a complete adolescent understanding of teenage lies and half-truths passed like telepathy across the table. "Yeah," Kurt said. "Totally. Like to be born again and all that, but with the Mormon Jesus, and the bread and the wine and the fish and the loaves."

My dad's lips opened, but Kurt went on, his right hand stroking the stubble on his dimpled chin: "I think I had a Mormon friend in junior high, or maybe he was Amish or Quaker. I can't remember. But what totally interests me about your church is all the wives, not that my friend's family was into that—only one mom—but that life really appeals to me: all the wives and kids. I've always wanted a big family. And don't you believe that you can become gods with all these superpowers?"

"Well, yes," my dad said, "but—"

"I'm totally behind it," Kurt said, "the long beard and the white robe, a throne with all my wives and kids around me. So cool." Kurt took a bite of pizza, chewing and speaking. "But not celebrating birthdays or Valentine's Day or Arbor Day? I don't know if I can commit to that."

"Kurt," my dad said, gripping the edge of the table with both hands, "the Mormon church doesn't practice polygamy anymore. That was almost a hundred years ago."

Kurt chewed his pizza and considered this. "You think they'll bring it back? I know a lot of guys who would join if they could have a few wives."

My dad's shoulders sank. The righteous zeal drained from his face. "Probably not, Kurt," he said.

Silence. Then Kurt's eyes drifted up to a painting that hung on the wall next to the table, a still life of a terra-cotta pot bursting with yellow poppies. It'd been there as long as I could remember, a relic from another life, a hobby my mom had, a distraction, she used to say, from her broken mind. Almost every wall in the house had one of her paintings: bowls of oranges and speckled red apples, vases spilling over with white tulips and pink carnations as big as my hands. I couldn't look at them.

"I like that painting," Kurt said.

My dad's jaw clenched. He gazed across the table, in my direction, but I knew he couldn't see me but something from long ago. "My wife painted it," he said. "Toby's mom." He smiled, a smile from another time. "Painting. She called it her therapy." My dad stared down at his plate. "She passed away in October."

As if something had called to me, I turned from the table to look into the dim living room where six circles, the size of half dollars, were pressed into the beige carpet. I'd tried to smooth them out with my hand, comb them out, run a vacuum over them, but they stayed: the imprints of the hospital bed where my mom lay for the last two weeks of her life.

I'd read something in my ninth-grade English class about how the mind's a dark forest. I guess that's how I made sense of it: that my mom got lost somewhere in her mind and couldn't find her way out. Worn down and scared for so many years, she just gave up and let herself waste away, even as my dad and I pleaded with her to take some water and a little soup—because that's all she needed to save her body. But she wouldn't.

It's hard to say "suicide," but I should probably call it what it is, even if there wasn't a bullet or a handful of pills or a crushing fall, and even if it took years of hospitals, psychiatrists, LA County social workers coming and going. There would be long stretches when she seemed like a normal mom, but always the eventual backslide, each time a little deeper into that forest until she wandered off, farther than she ever had, and never came out.

And where did all her pain go? As far as I could tell, she left it behind for me and my dad. I guess that's why I'd tried not to think about her.

I looked at Kurt. He had one elbow on the table, his chin on his palm, that white plastic bracelet touching the tattered edge of his shirtsleeve. He'd followed my gaze to the carpet, and then he smiled, like he could see right into me.

And that look never left Kurt's face as he sang "Happy Birthday" along with my dad and Scotty and as I blew out the candles and my dad dropped huge slices of mango cheesecake onto our plates. And that smile was still there when we finished the cake and Kurt said, "We should jam together."

I felt a rush hit my brain. "Can we?" I asked my dad.

I looked at Scotty. He was practically panting.

"I don't know." My dad frowned at his watch. "It's a school night."

But then I played another card. "I thought maybe on my birthday it would be all right. Just this once."

My dad's arms flopped to his side. "Okay," he said. "But not too late."

▪■■▪

We led Kurt down a narrow staircase to a room in the basement where we stored our Christmas decorations. All our equipment was down there: Scotty's drum kit, my Fender Squire and Epiphone acoustic, two Peavey amps, and a mic duct-taped to a wobbly stand we found at Goodwill.

"This is it," I said, knowing Kurt might appreciate the yellow linoleum and the bleak bone-white of the overhead fluorescent lighting, all in hilarious contrast to the fake Christmas tree and 40-inch plastic Santa Claus in the far corner of the room.

Kurt raised up onto his tiptoes and poked a water-stained ceiling tile. "The shittier the better," he said.

I lifted my Fender Squier and held it out to Kurt, hoping that something of him might absorb into the guitar. "You working on anything?" I couldn't help asking.

Kurt reached for the guitar and eased the strap over his shoulder. I flipped the amps on.

"That's what everyone wants to know," Kurt said into the microphone, his amplified voice filling the room. "There's some rumor about a blues album, but that's bullshit. You want to know something?" Kurt twisted the guitar's tuning pegs, smirking with some secret knowledge. "Truth is, I've written one song in the last six months, one depressing little piece of shit." Upstairs, a toilet flushed. Water rushed through a pipe somewhere above the stained ceiling tiles. "You want to hear it?" he asked, not looking at us, like he thought we might turn him down.

Scotty and I nodded dumbly in unison, feeling stupid and pathetic, like we'd synchronized it.

Kurt started strumming, a fast up and down in a minor key that sent a sudden shiver across my chest and down my back, that eerie feeling of peering into empty rooms or at old grainy photos. I leaned in, hoping for a key change, for Kurt to tap the fuzz pedal and lift the song from its sad groove. I waited for the stinging lyrics, something quintessentially Nirvana, the shocking, incongruous images, the railing social commentary against the phonies and the wannabes.

Then Kurt stepped up to the mic, his voice groaning out of him, like a deep ache as he sang, something about a son who'd tried again and again to make his parents proud. I looked at Scotty, his faded navy Vans tapping time with the downbeat, his smile until, absorbing the words, his foot slowed and then stopped. He slumped into one of the lawn chairs we kept in the room and stared down at the pattern of dizzying loops and swirls in the yellow linoleum. And I was hunched over in one of the lawn chairs, too, though I couldn't remember sitting. My right hand covered my mouth.

Kurt let the final chord ring until the strings stopped vibrating. Scotty swallowed hard and then stood up. He looked at me and then back to Kurt.

"Next album?" is all Scotty could say.

Kurt ran his hand across the short stubble on his cheeks. He didn't look at us, but at something above our heads. "No, that one's just for me."

The three of us stood there. The amps buzzed. Kurt shook his head. "Fuck," he said. "It's your birthday." He struck a major chord. "Let's play something."

Scotty didn't hesitate, reaching his drum kit in three long steps. I was at my Epiphone acoustic in two, throwing the strap over my shoulder. And when I brushed my pick over the strings and they sounded right, I looked at Scotty, his two raised fists ready to lay into the snare drum and hi-hats.

"How about 'Smoke on the Water'?" Kurt said. "Or 'Wild Thing'?"

"How about 'Teen Spirit'?" I said.

Kurt groaned. "Oh, God, aren't you sick of that fucking song?" He looked over at Scotty and then at me. Scotty's hair was wild, his eyes swelling from the sockets. I must have looked about the same.

Kurt smiled. "You two look fucking pathetic." He played an F minor, the song's first unmistakable chord. "You know it?" Kurt asked, and I laughed at that because not to know it—not to have strummed along a thousand times with Kurt as his voice wailed from the speakers in my room—would have been unforgivable to anyone at school who played guitar.

A thin blush rose through Kurt's patchy scruff. "Okay," he said. And then he counted to three, and together we played those first four chords, and it was like hearing the song for the first time, when its gravity pulled me toward the radio, a sound I'd never heard before, the wrecking ball that toppled all those stupid eighties hair bands. A clean electric sound filled the room until Kurt tapped the fuzz pedal with his right foot and a booming static erupted from the amp. That's when Scotty, right on cue, laid into the snare drum. And I was right there with Kurt, my left hand a blur against the bronze strings and black pickguard. I looked at Kurt and, in an instant, he'd become what I wanted him to be. Not that pissed off, worn-out rock star chain smoking in the back of my car but the Kurt Cobain I'd meticulously studied in all that MTV concert footage, that slight straddle, his whole body swaying forward and back, soaked through with the pure thrill of the music. And right before Kurt stepped to the mic and I lost his face behind that curtain of blond hair, he looked at me and smiled, a benevolent, big-hearted smile.

▪■▪■▪

It was past eleven when we drove Kurt—conked out in the backseat, head against the window, arms hugging his body—to LAX. I didn't want the radio on. Whatever KROQ was pumping out at that hour would only dilute the raw sound looping through my brain, Kurt's voice, its energy. I wanted to savor it before time grabbed it away.

I looked at Scotty, an outline in the darkness momentarily illuminated by the towering lights above the 405, his lips moving but with no sound, this strange moment like a sweet, fleeting flavor on his tongue.

Kurt didn't stir as we pulled to the curb in front of the airport terminal. "Hey," Scotty whispered, shaking Kurt's knee. Kurt's eyes snapped open. He squinted up at the glaring terminal lights. A few stray hairs were smeared across his damp forehead, and two thin lines of snot leaked from his nostrils.

"Well," Kurt said, flashing that sly rock star smile, "you think anyone will believe you, the fucking night you hung out with Kurt Cobain?" He was fighting for that smile. Whatever he had surging through his veins earlier was almost used up.

Kurt pulled the crumpled directions to that cinder block apartment from his shirt pocket. "You got a pen?" He tore the paper into two ragged halves.

Scotty dove for the glove compartment, pushing through CD cases and wadded Kleenex, until he pulled out a dull pencil.

Kurt scratched his name on the two halves and handed them over the seat. Scotty held his, absorbed in tracing Kurt's signature with his finger.

Then Kurt unclipped the silver chain from his wallet and belt loop. "Happy birthday," he said.

The chain swung from Kurt's thumb, the same chain I'd seen bouncing on his hip in concert footage from The Paramount and Live and Loud. It seemed too personal, an extension of his body. I shook my head. "I can't."

"Take it." Kurt took my hand and dropped the chain into my damp palm.

I held it, hefting its cool weight, and before I could stop myself, I asked, "What about you?" I was really asking about the hotel room in Rome and the cinder block apartment and the plastic bracelet on Kurt's wrist. "We can take you back." I held my breath. My heart pounded. "If you want."

The skin around Kurt's eyes tightened, the briefest flash of annoyance, Kurt's rebel spirit rising. But then his eyes softened. "No, I'm a fucking hopeless case. Always have been," he said, opening the door and stepping onto the curb. He turned and leaned into the car. "Hey, your mom's paintings," he said, "they're pretty awesome. Beautiful. It's cool she left them for you."

And with that, Kurt walked into the terminal, the light there as bright as the noonday sun, and when I blinked, I saw Kurt's thin, white outline against the black backdrop of my closed eyelids before the image burned out.

"I'm framing this," Scotty said, stroking Kurt's signature with his fingertips.

I leaned forward until my head rested on the steering wheel. I thought of all my mom's paintings, and how I couldn't look at them without seeing her shrunken face against a white pillow. I suddenly knew Kurt was wrong. Where was the beauty there? I didn't see it.

I opened the car door and walked into the terminal. I heard Scotty through the open window. "Hey," he shouted. But I didn't turn. The terminal doors opened with a blast of warm air that shot down on me. I was moving quickly toward Kurt, my steps strangely loud in the near-empty terminal.

"Kurt," I said. He turned. I was suddenly self-conscious. He was no longer part of my world but had returned to his, the rock star on the cover of *Rolling Stone*, the subject of a thousand rumors, the rebel voice of a generation. Three screens above us, all those arrivals and departures, cast a yellow light onto the polished floor. A man and woman studying the rows of departing flights, not much older than Kurt, both in red flannel shirts, torn jeans, and Doc Marten boots, looked at us. A soft gasp squeaked through the woman's lips. She leaned toward the man and whispered in his ear.

"I'd rather have her than all those paintings," I told Kurt. My voice slipped. Something broke up and stirred in my chest, some old feeling. "All that pain she had," I said. "Maybe she didn't even realize it. Maybe she thought she'd take it with her. But it just stays behind."

Kurt didn't say anything. He didn't move, and his face at that moment—framed by his long, greasy hair, his eyes almost in shadow—is forever fixed in my mind. He looked at me, but I wasn't sure he saw me or something else, maybe some scene playing out in his mind. His stubbled chin dropped to his chest, and he twisted his head away from me until I couldn't see his face. Then he turned and walked away.

"Is that Kurt Cobain?" the woman asked. She wore a black Alice in Chains tour shirt under the unbuttoned flannel. The man stood at her side, licking his lips, waiting for me to say something. His red flannel shirt had an ironed crease running up each sleeve, and the black Doc Martens didn't have a scuff or mark on the leather, like they'd just come out of a box. In six months, in a year, they'd be wearing something else, listening to something else.

"Fuck off," I said, and walked away.

In the car, Scotty sat there, still mesmerized by Kurt's autograph. "I'm bringing this to school. I'm showing it to everyone." He raised the thin scrap of paper to his nose and sniffed its edges. "What'd you say to him?"

I gripped the steering wheel, the engine's idle vibrating through my arms.

Deep in my right pocket, I felt the weight of Kurt's wallet chain. "I don't think he's all right," I said. But Scotty didn't hear me. He was humming something, tapping his heels against the floor mats, still staring at Kurt's signature as I pulled away from the terminal curb.

The 405 and 101 swarmed with an absurd midnight traffic as we crawled toward Burbank. My dad would be pissed. So would Scotty's parents. I'd probably lose the car for a month. But I didn't care. As the exits ticked past, I tried clearing my throat a few times and looking over at Scotty. I wanted to talk about what happened, to make sense of it. But Scotty never looked up, his eyes fixed on Kurt's signature, never saying a word, even as I pulled into his driveway. He opened the car door, heaved it shut, and disappeared into the house.

That night a space opened between us until we drifted apart at the end of the summer, me to Brigham Young University and soon after to a Mormon mission in Chicago, and Scotty to start a band with some guys from Burbank High. Within a couple years, they built a following around Los Angeles. KROQ featured them twice as a New Pick of the Week, and then they were playing the Whiskey and the Troubadour. And then they had a record deal, appearances on *The Late Show* and *Conan*, and last I heard they were opening for The Shins. But before all that, I don't think Scotty ever forgave me for that Friday morning he showed up to school with Kurt's autograph in a cheap black plastic frame and a story so incredible that our friends laughed to tears, but I didn't back him up. I never talked about it then—because no one would have believed us, anyway. The truth is that something profound happened that night, yet its meaning that Friday morning hovered just beyond my reach, and to even bring it up felt wrong. But Scotty never understood that. All he saw from that night was a story.

■■■

Sunday, April 10. I watched Kurt's memorial on MTV, five thousand kids at the Seattle Center lighting candles and wiping tears as Courtney Love read Kurt's suicide note.

I was in the kitchen Friday morning when I'd heard the news on KROQ's Kevin and Bean Show: "Shotgun wound to the head . . . body found at home . . . suicide note . . . untimely death." And when I heard it, I remember looking over at the table, at the cushioned chair Kurt had sat in, then up at the yellow poppies my mom had painted. Then I was sitting on the kitchen floor, the tiles cold through my jeans. I sensed a familiar, sad anger in me. Once again, I was arriving at a line of demarcation in my life, something ending and something new and unknown beginning.

I was angry as Courtney read that note, at what Kurt had done to himself. I could hardly believe what she read, in Kurt's own words: how he couldn't feel the music anymore, his guilt for going through the motions night after night on stage. And hearing that, it was hard to be angry. I thought of Kurt in my basement, an image as vivid today as it was then, only six days from his end, strung out on heroin, hating life, hopeless, numb. Yet, his eyes closed, hair damp with sweat, body thrashing with the music, Kurt's last performance: a gift.

When the memorial ended, I walked into the kitchen and turned on the radio. Green Day's "Longview," on heavy rotation for the last month, was ending, the bass line fading out. A window was open. Birds whistled in the backyard. Ecstatic voices barked from the radio: a new furniture store in Glendale; a sale at JCPenney; lower insurance rates for safe drivers. Any moment the music would start again—all those songs, the soundtrack of my teenage life. But I understood how, from that moment, they would never quite sound the same.

Light Departure

for Doug Thayer

Near the end of my mission, I'd often catch myself thinking about what to take home from Italy—and what I wouldn't take home. I'd think about it as I knocked doors and stopped people on Ravenna's narrow cobblestone streets, my eyes drifting to the arched windows of high-end clothes boutiques where faceless mannequins stood in Dolce & Gabbana suits. What to take home? What had other missionaries taken home? Designer shoes and ties. Murano glass. Amateur paintings of the Tuscan countryside and the Grand Canal. I had my eye on a pair of Gucci loafers and some Brioni ties, which I finally bought in the last weeks of my mission with money my parents sent me. I had this image of myself after the mission, striking a charming, cosmopolitan pose—*la bella figura*, as Italians called it—at church and on dates, in a navy-blue silk tie and shoes whose polished leather glowed like caramel. I'd also amassed, thanks to Italy's lax copyright laws, more than sixty rare bootlegs, enough to fill three shoeboxes: Nirvana, Pearl Jam, Led Zeppelin, The Doors—all bands I'd loved in high school. But how to get it all home?

To free up space in my suitcase, I'd decided to throw out most of the clothes I'd brought into the mission. Two years of walking and riding bikes had practically destroyed them. The lining of my wool suit jacket was in tatters, my dress slacks were frayed around the cuffs and the belt loops, and my shirts, once a brilliant white, were tinged a dull yellow and had a musty odor that never washed out. Still, packing for home the night before I was to take an early express train to the mission home in Padova, I set aside a pair of slacks and two shirts. I wanted my dad and my brothers, all returned missionaries who'd done their time, to see in the battered clothes my hard work.

Across the room, my companion, Carr, was sprawled over his twin bed, an open Bible propped up on his chest, the whole great bulk of him sunk into the cheap mattress. As I dropped a handful of socks into an open black trash bag at my feet, he watched me through wire-framed glasses, his face red, as if he'd just exerted himself. I could tell he was pissed off about something.

Carr had a real distaste for anything wasteful. He refused to throw out the leftover pasta from our lunches, eating it at night, cold and congealed, out of what seemed more a sense of duty than enjoyment. I'd even seen him pinch specks of green mold from his bread rather than throw it out.

"You should give those clothes to someone," he finally said, his mouth a gaping, disapproving hole. His gray eyes looked cartoonishly big.

I held a pair of gray slacks to my hips. "You want them? Just your size." I swayed my hips and winked, a ridiculous offer, a joke Carr wouldn't get. He easily had me by five inches and a hundred and fifty pounds.

Carr turned back to the Bible on his chest. "No thanks."

"And who'd want them?" I asked, balling up the slacks before dropping them into the trash bag.

Carr peered at me over the Bible, only his magnified eyes and pimpled forehead visible to me. His voice, muffled by the pages, came to me faintly. "What about that guy from Senegal who sells CDs?"

"What guy from Senegal?" I had no idea who he was talking about.

"The guy in Piazza del Popolo. His clothes are all torn up and dirty."

I stripped another pair of slacks from a hanger. "I give some African street vendor a couple of white shirts and pants and suddenly every Italian thinks the Mormon missionaries are in the bootleg business. Should I give him my nametag, too?"

Carr shrugged. "I just think it's wasteful, throwing away all those clothes."

"Of course you do," I said. I lifted a stack of thick missionary reference books from my nightstand—books I'd brought into the mission and carried dutifully from city to city with each transfer, soon realizing that each apartment had dozens of them tucked away in closets and drawers, discarded by homebound missionaries. For a moment, I considered adding mine to the trash bag but felt Carr's heavy gaze. Instead, I slid the books to the back of the closet, between a single rusted barbell and a pair of dusty rubber galoshes.

With a wheezy grunt, Carr hefted himself off the bed and moved toward the light switch. I watched his slow, heavy-footed progress across the room, always the same unhurried gait, even when we were late for a teaching appointment. He had to be the heaviest elder in the mission, his doughy belly straining the buttons of his white shirt, its wrinkled tail refusing to stay tucked in. Even his features seemed doughy, his glasses sinking into the soft, pale flesh around his eyes, a clefted roll of neck fat bulging over his collar.

I'd cataloged my frustrations with Carr in letters to my best friend, Eric Rigby, who was on his mission in Buenos Aires. I noted Carr's long-winded rambling with me and his deathly silence around strangers, an obsession with train schedules, bouts with kidney stones that kept him in bed for days at a time, and an irritating compulsion to pocket rocks and bits of trash that interested him. I also bemoaned Carr's hour-long morning showers, admitting to Eric that I'd taken to pissing in the kitchen sink rather than pound on the bathroom door to hurry Carr along. I knew Eric would find all this amusing. I speculated as to the reason for Carr's marathon showers. Napping? Self-pleasure? Though I finally revealed to Eric that the fantasy novel I'd discovered tucked into Carr's folded towel might offer an explanation.

In response, Eric sent a crude sketch of Carr as a huge, lumbering sloth with Coke-bottle glasses and a dopey smile, soaking in a steamy bubble bath, a long bristled brush in one clawed hand and a book in the other. In the sketch, I stood at the bathroom door, bent over double, cupping my crotch with both hands, a pinched expression of excruciating pain on my face. Now, watching Carr plod across the room, I had to bite my cheek to hold back a giggle, almost unable not to see him as a goofy sloth.

"Are we working tonight?" Carr asked. It was early evening and the room had filled with a dusky light. "If not, I'm going to bed."

Carr flipped the light switch. Then he returned slowly to his bed, the metal frame trembling as he sat and reached for his shoelaces.

"No, we're working," I said. I knew if Carr took even a shoe off, there'd be no getting him out of the apartment that night. He'd hunker down in bed with a fantasy novel tucked behind his Bible and soon be snoring. "Twenty minutes," I said, "and then we'll go."

I looked out the window above my bed, at the sunset reflecting off the terracotta roof of the Museo Nazionale, and beyond that to the Adriatic Sea, a gray ribbon below a blue-ochre sky.

On my last night in Ravenna, I wanted to stroll the cobblestone streets with a *gelato* in my hand, past the Mercado Coperto, and then stand in front of the Basilica di San Vitale one last time to admire its stepped towers and arched windows. Most nights I'd chosen a route back to our apartment that passed by the ancient church. I always felt something profound and instructive there when I contemplated the pitted bricks and the marble chapel steps worn by countless feet. Fifteen centuries of snow and sun and rain, wars and invasions, the fall and rise of empires, and the church still stood.

One Saturday, the basilica's organist, a squat, gray-haired man who smelled like sweat and alcohol, curious about our black nametags, stopped us outside the church. When I asked what the church's mosaics looked like from the organ loft, the man winked and said cryptically, "I'll let you in on a secret."

We followed him up a dim, steep staircase into the basilica's narrow organ loft, where suddenly the bright Byzantine mosaics, so close now, loomed before us: scenes of pious prophets and winged cherubs and the hand of God reaching through billowing clouds, all in brilliant color and intricate detail. I felt dazed by the beauty.

The man pointed to the ceiling and whispered, "Perhaps the most famous mosaics in the world, but see how some of them are painted on." He gazed at the tourists below, shaking his head. "And look at the dumb sheep down there. They have no idea."

As if his words had broken a spell, I suddenly saw how large sections of the ceiling were painted on. With this revelation, I felt my jaw loosen and drop.

I turned to Carr, who barely glanced up, seemingly unconcerned as he gnawed at a hangnail on his thumb.

The falseness of those painted-on mosaics bothered me. I wanted to see the ancient church one last time, from the outside, to remember its looming bell tower and solid walls, the way the ground lights shining on the old brick radiated an amber glow, and not think about those painted-on mosaics inside.

Carr's bed frame shuddered and squeaked as he stood and moved to his desk. "Did I show you the kidney stone I passed last week?" he asked. "Or what about this one?" He opened a Ziploc bag, pinched a tiny jagged stone between his fingers, then raised it to the light as if he were a jeweler appraising a fine diamond. "I passed this one in my last city. It was stuck in my urethra all night because I didn't have any more liquids in me to pee it out. Want to hold it?"

I felt my body recoil from Carr's outstretched hand. "No," I said.

Carr rolled the stone between his thumb and index finger before dropping it back into the bag. "My girlfriend has kidney stones too," he said. "Isn't that strange? Maybe it's a sign we're meant to be together. But, I mean, there's more than just that. We both collect Pokémon cards and love Robert Jordan's *The Wheel of Time* series. We're also writing a fantasy novel in long verse. And we both have an allergy to peanuts and a birthmark on our knuckles, though Bria's is on her right hand. Sure, we want to get married, eventually, but her parents think we should finish college first. They think a woman should be financially independent. I totally agree. That's why Bria wants to open a rescue shelter for homeless parrots."

"Homeless parrots?" I said. "Sounds like she's really getting in on the ground floor. Plenty of earning potential." I waited for Carr to grasp my wisecrack, a smile or chuckle, but nothing.

He lifted a piece of thin copper wire from the desk and began twisting it into a pair of circular wings. Dozens of his wire creatures covered the desk, dragons, eagles, wolves, and tigers carefully placed around stacked books and pens and pencils. "She's not in it for the money," Carr said. "Parrots can live like fifty years. All the time they outlive their owners. And then there's no one to take care of them."

Carr had transformed the piece of wire into a butterfly, holding it in one hand and a wire dragon in the other, whipping them through the air in wide loops, as if they were battling, his lips vibrating with the sounds of explosions, lasers, and agonizing screams.

Carr wasn't at all how I imagined the last months of my mission. I assumed that I'd train a new missionary and continue on as a zone leader. I'd even considered that the mission president might call me as one of his assistants. So when President Martinson phoned unexpectedly the night before transfers, I experienced a sudden burst of light-headed excitement, which quickly dissolved when he told me that Carr would be my last companion. And with that news, the phone pressed to my ear, I felt as if a weight was suddenly bearing down on me, almost forcing a groan through my lips.

"Elder Carr has his quirks," President Martinson had told me. His voice sounded distant and dreamy, like he was remembering something amusing about Carr. He laughed dryly, but stopped, and when he continued, there was a little catch his voice. "But I've never met anyone as loving and without guile," President Martinson said. "I know he's not easy to live with. He needs some confidence and motivation. He needs someone to keep him focused. I was hoping you could help."

The arrangement sounded more like babysitting, but I agreed, feeling some of the gloomy weight lift when I understood that President Martinson had sought me out, deemed me competent and reliable enough to undertake this difficult assignment.

Carr looked up from his wire creations and yawned. "I'm tired," he said.

"Ten minutes," I said, "and then we'll leave."

That night, our last as a companionship, I wanted to say something kind to Carr about our time together, just as I'd done with my other companions, but I didn't know what to say. The truth was that nothing about Carr interested me, and that had made our two months together seem endless and uneventful, the minutes and hours prolonged by boredom as we walked the streets and knocked doors, Carr blathering from one subject to the next. Bria. Conan the Barbarian. Time travel. Vampires. Kidney stones. With my other companions, there'd always been some common ground: college football, old girlfriends, the pretty girls we'd seen that day, or all the silliness, big games, and hilarious pranks from high school. But it wasn't just the boredom with Carr. He annoyed me with his self-righteousness and quiet judgment, which he handed down with weighty silences, innuendo, and looks of mild disgust.

I'd liked all of my companions, sure, and had learned something from each one. But what had I learned from Carr? Maybe patience and how to keep my mouth shut rather than say something disparaging. The truth was that I couldn't wait to board that express train in the morning, to be done with Carr, finally untethered and free from all his strangeness.

I lifted a shoebox from my dresser and carefully balanced it on my palm, savoring the solid weight of the handmade Gucci loafers inside.

"You wearing those home?" Carr asked, pointing to the shoebox with the wire butterfly.

I raised a foot to show him my black Wingtips. "I'm wearing what I brought into the mission." The shoe's finish had worn away over the toes, and the rubber heel had eroded to a sharp angle.

I set the open shoebox at the end of my bed so I could admire the Guccis' bright silver buckles and smell the new leather as I packed. The shoes seemed to radiate light, the color somehow reminding me of San Vitale's weathered brick.

"When's your homecoming talk?" Carr asked.

"Sunday," I said, sliding a thick stack of letters from Eric and a few other friends into the outside pocket of my suitcase.

"Sunday?" Carr's eyes bulged. "This Sunday? Have you written anything? What are you going to say?"

"It'll come to me," I said, as if I weren't at all worried—though for the past month, with a growing anxiety, I'd often thought about what I'd say to my congregation.

My older brother, Marc, who'd returned from Guadalajara a year before I left for Italy, told story after story of the people he'd baptized, repentant drug dealers and bottomed-out alcoholics, families who'd dreamed of him and his companion knocking on their doors—stories that had brought tears to my eyes and drawn me to the edge of the pew as he'd recounted them in his homecoming talk.

I didn't have a reserve of inspiring stories. At best, I had one story that might impress my ward, the conversion of a man named Michael Ono, a young Nigerian refugee who'd eagerly invited me and my first companion into his tenement apartment on the outskirts of Bologna.

We'd sat at a wobbly card table drinking chamomile tea and talking. Michael, arms folded and rocking himself slightly, had a hungry, disoriented look. He was shorter than me and had the body of a distance runner, his thin frame lost in a pair of secondhand purple warm-up pants and a faded red sweatshirt whose sleeves were so long that only his fingertips were visible. Like Michael's clothes, everything in the apartment seemed mismatched, the worn furniture and the pots and pans that hung above the sink, even the chipped teacups we held. I remembered thinking that there was a humility about him, something almost effeminate, yet refreshingly different from the bravado and dirty jokes we often encountered when stopping Italian men on the streets.

Michael recounted his journey to Italy on a crowded Libyan fishing boat with two hundred other passengers. As I listened, the radiator in the kitchen gurgled and hissed, and the cramped apartment seemed enveloped in a stifling tropical heat and the pungent odor of exotic spices. I felt the need to stand and shed my heavy wool coat, but I didn't want to interrupt or miss a word as Michael stared intently at the card table's stained top, as if in a trance, describing how the smugglers beat them when they complained of heat and thirst, and how two older Somali women suffocated to death below deck and were thrown overboard. When the engines failed and the smugglers abandoned the boat, Michael had survived for three days on only toothpaste and rainwater, until the Italian Navy rescued the passengers. He'd spent two weeks at a relocation facility in Sicily and was then sent to northern Italy. He lived in Bologna but worked at a shoe factory near Forlì.

Before we left Michael's apartment that day, he agreed to meet the next evening. A month later he was baptized.

That was almost two years ago.

I thumbed through a stack of Michael's letters before setting them in my suitcase. After I left Bologna, we'd written monthly. Soon, though, Michael's letters came sporadically, every two months and then three, and by the time I came to Ravenna, he hadn't written in months. I'd tried his number in Bologna but found it disconnected.

Someone knocked at the apartment door. The wire butterfly slipped from Carr's thick fingers and bounced on the wooden desk. He sat up straight and looked at me.

"Maybe that girl again," I said. "I think she's in love with you."

At least once a week a teenage girl from across the hall, always heavily made up and in a tight, low-cut T-shirt, knocked at our door. To practice her English, she'd tell us, as she grilled us about life in America and if we had girlfriends and if we ever felt sexually repressed by all the rules we had to follow.

There was another knock, this time louder and more insistent. I winked at Carr. "It's all that manliness you give off. Why don't you see what she wants?"

Carr pressed his hand to his chest. "Hey, I've never even talked to her. I don't even look at her." His voice cracked. "Maybe you should go. I wouldn't know what to say."

I lifted my suitcase, testing its weight. "Confidence," I said.

Carr groaned as he stood and left the bedroom. But he returned quickly.

"She try putting the moves on you?" I asked.

"No. It's some black guy," Carr whispered. "He says he knows you. Michael, I think."

I looked up from the suitcase. "Michael? I baptized him in Bologna. Tell him to come in."

"We're not supposed to let anyone in," Carr said, fingering the corner of the small mission rulebook in his breast pocket.

"You want to tell him that?" I asked. "A new convert. A new member of the church." I straightened my tie in the full-length mirror next to my bed, frowning at Carr's reflection. "You want to tell him to have a seat in the hallway, elder?"

"Fine," Carr said.

And then Michael was there, smiling as he long-stepped across the room with his hand extended. "Elder Allred," he said. "A prayer answered. At this hour, I didn't think you'd be home. I was ready to walk the streets searching for you."

"I can't believe it," I said, shaking Michael's hand. His presence felt unreal. I hardly recognized him. He wore some kind of traditional African clothing, a long blue shirt embroidered with gold thread around the neck and the sleeves, loose-fitting pants, and a black, flat-topped hat.

"What a surprise," I said. "And you." I touched the gold embroidery on Michael's sleeve. "What's this?"

"A gift from my parents," Michael said. "A *dashiki*. Very popular in West Africa, very comfortable in the summers, though the Italians hate when I wear it. Too colorful. Too ethnic. I suddenly become a suspicious person. We work in their factories and pick up their trash, but they don't want to see us." Michael stepped back to look at me. "And you. More grown up. You were still a boy in Bologna."

"I send pictures home and my parents say the same thing." I slid the chair from my desk toward Michael and then sat on the end of my bed. "You've met my companion, Elder Carr."

Michael sat, placing both hands on his knees. "I have," he said. He tipped his head toward Carr. "A pleasure."

Carr was back on his bed, the Bible again propped up on his chest. He'd slipped on a yellow sweatshirt, raising its peaked hood. The hood cast a shadow over his broad face.

I felt the need to explain Carr's silence. "Elder Carr isn't a big talker around people he doesn't know," I said, loud enough for Carr to hear. "But he's working on it. Right, Carr?"

"Perhaps this silence is a virtue," Michael said, turning to Carr. "Wisdom is the reward of listening. My mother always told me that." Michael turned back to me, his gaze falling on my open suitcase. "So I arrived in time. A few days ago I ran into the Bologna missionaries outside the train station. When I asked about you, they said you leave tomorrow. I had to say goodbye." Michael pointed to my suitcase. "You're ready for the journey?"

I ran my finger along the edge of the open shoebox. "Almost," I said.

"And these shoes," Michael asked. "These beautiful shoes are yours?"

I lifted one from the box. "A gift to myself. Something to remember Italy by."

"May I?" Michael asked.

I passed the shoe to him. "You like them?"

Michael held the loafer with both hands. "Yes, very much." He turned the shoe slowly. "Double monk-strap, Goodyear welting, hand-stitched calfskin, and look at the detailing on the leather. Expensive. You'll make quite an impression."

"You still work in that shoe factory?" I asked.

"Not anymore," Michael said, examining the shoe's leather sole. "But I learned a lot there, more than I care to about something I could never afford. I also learned that *Made in Italy* really means *Made in Italy by Africans.* Nigerians, Kenyans, Moroccans, Somalis. Every day at work was like an African Union Summit, but instead of debating economics and politics we made shoes." He handed the shoe to me. "Now I make couches. All very boring, but the factory's closer to my apartment. And it pays more. You didn't get my letters?"

"Not for the last four months," I said. "I began to think you went back to Nigeria."

Michael slapped his knee. "Why am I still shocked by the incompetence of the Italian Post when every morning I see my mail carrier in the café drinking espresso and reading *la Repubblica*? I moved apartments three months ago and am still waiting for my forwarded mail. But in the great scheme of things, these are small problems." Michael rubbed his palms together. "What's important is that you'll soon be with your family."

"Only for a couple weeks," I said, "and then I'm off to Brigham Young University."

"Wonderful," Michael said. His eyes moved to the ceiling. "Praise God. All is well when we let him take control." He touched his chest and smiled a sly grin. "And I, too, have some good news. I've won a visa to America. Fifteen million applicants and I was one of fifty thousand. I still can't believe it. In two months I interview with the American Embassy in Milan. If all goes well, I'll be in America by November. Can you believe this miracle, Allred? An American citizen. God is faithful, isn't he?"

"A blessing," I said, almost in a whisper. "You deserve it. After all you've been through."

"A new beginning, yet so many unknowns," Michael said, the energy draining from his voice. "I'd be a fool to think I can start a new life alone. By nature I'm prideful, but I mustn't let pride bring me low. Maybe what I ask is too much, Allred. Forgive me if it is, and then we'll never speak of it again. But you once showed me a picture of your parents' house. Big and beautiful. Plenty of rooms. I was hoping I might stay with them for a month or so. I'll be a mouse, but not even a squeak. I can help. I can clean. I've read that there's opportunity in Seattle. Colleges. Jobs. Just until I find work and an apartment. I'll pay them back."

I was touched by Michael's request. On Sunday, I imagined myself standing at the pulpit in front of my congregation, recounting Michael's story: a man fleeing the political and religious unrest of his country for a better life, the treacherous journey at sea, a refugee in a foreign land, his conversion, and now this miraculous golden ticket to a new life in America. And then a few months later Michael would be there among my congregation, smiling, shaking hands, the very fruit of my mission. That Michael would come to my apartment the night before I was to leave Italy; that, against incredible odds, he'd won this visa; that I could help him build a life in America—all this seemed beyond coincidence. It seemed like the hand of God.

"Of course I'll speak with my parents," I said. "I've told them about you. How could they say no?"

I looked over at Carr on his bed. His black socks had fallen around his chucky ankles, exposing his goose-pimpled skin. I hoped he was listening, hoped he understood this is how he needed to love and serve others, by opening up rather than crawling into himself.

"Thank you," Michael said softly, letting out a long breath. "God will bless you." He interlaced his fingers and touched them to his forehead.

"Though I'm sure the members in Bologna will miss you," I said. "How are they? The Rossi family? Brother Pavone?"

Michael stared at his interlocked fingers. "Honestly, I haven't been to church in a long time," he said. "Many months."

My stomach tightened. "Was there a problem? You didn't feel welcome?"

"Nothing like that," Michael said. "Everyone was kind. It's just that I've changed. My life has changed, my beliefs. I cannot pretend to be something I am not. I cannot be something different from how God created me."

"I don't understand." I could hear my voice ticking higher, an undercurrent of panic there I had to check. "You have doubts?" I suddenly felt the need to teach Michael, just as I'd done in his small apartment, to quote scripture and bear testimony, to answer questions and resolve concerns.

"It's because of somebody I met," Michael said, "somebody I love deeply. I cannot be with him and be Mormon. And I want to be with him."

A noisy motor scooter passed on the street below, but its shrill whine didn't seem to penetrate the silence in the room. I could feel the clunky thud of my heart. I picked a loose thread from my luggage and worked it between my thumb and index finger until it formed a tight ball. I let it fall through my fingertips. I'd known, perhaps intuitively, from the very first time I met Michael. "You're gay?" I asked.

"Perhaps I've always been," Michael said. "I remember in grade school, a feeling whenever I saw an attractive boy. Why did I find boys attractive? I thought God had made a mistake. Maybe my father suspected. He pushed me to sports. Soccer, boxing, running. But the feeling wouldn't go away. As a teenager, I told my pastor. The demon, he called it. He made me promise never to tell anyone. He told me to pray and read the Bible, to cover my private parts when bathing. But still those feelings. In Nigeria, people talk about gays with such disgust. And in the news, beatings, killings. I thought of a new start. I would leave the demon there. That's what I told myself. That's why I let you in my apartment. A new faith, a new beginning. But really, I wouldn't admit then that I left Nigeria to find the freedom to be myself."

I leaned forward, elbows on my knees. I wanted to fix Michael, to say words that would steer him back, yet I felt something in me sinking, moving beyond my grasp. "You have to pray for strength to overcome this," I said.

"And I believed that, too." Michael spoke slowly, patiently, as if he were now teaching me. "But how can this love be wrong? Abasi. That's his name, a Kenyan who knows what I know about the shame and loneliness of hiding a secret. With him, I feel only acceptance. We've found a community in Bologna, other Africans and Italians like us. Christians. There's so much love there, Allred."

Michael looked at the floor. "I know this isn't what you expected, Allred, but to be dishonest, to hide, is weakness. After meeting Abasi, I vowed to no longer live a lie. No more shame and guilt." A faint chime sounded. Michael frowned at the silver watch on his wrist. "This is a lot to tell you. I wish there was more time, but I must go. The last train to Bologna will leave soon. I must work tomorrow." Michael stood and pulled a slip of paper from his pants pocket. "My email and cell number. You can write or call after you speak to your parents. Please, tell them I won't be a burden. Tell them it will only be for a short time." Michael stared down at the paper that hung between us. "But if the arrangement doesn't work, if circumstances change, I understand. It will never change my gratitude. The lessons. Your letters. Your friendship, Allred. You helped me through dark times, brother." Michael touched my shoulder. "It's late and you're still packing. I'll let myself out." He nodded to Carr before turning to leave.

I listened to Michael's footsteps in the hallway, and then to the heavy opening and closing of the apartment door. Carr was still on his bed, the open Bible now fallen across his belly. I thought he might be asleep.

I stared at the slip of paper in my hand, suddenly resentful, feeling manipulated by Michael's talk of needing me to start a new life in America, and then his revelation—abandoning the faith, loving a man—after I agreed to help. I sensed something new in Michael that I didn't like: the conspicuous tribal clothes, the hint of political activism, a lack of humility and meekness. I moved my thumb over the neat rows of letters and numbers Michael had written in blue ink. The thin paper felt weightless. I imagined it falling through my fingers, vanishing under the bed or behind the nightstand, and ceasing to exist. And with that thought, I looked at Carr, motionless on his bed, his chest rising and falling rhythmically.

From the top shelf of my closet, I took a pair of black knit gloves I had no intention of taking home, and let them fall, along with the slip of paper, into the trash bag.

"Your parents will say yes, right? They'll let him stay for a month. Just for a month."

Carr's voice, his eager rush of words, startled me.

I turned to him. His face was shadowed from the sweatshirt's hood. He now sat on the edge of the bed, bent toward me. The peaked hood gave him the look of a ghoulish inquisitor.

I could see the slip of paper peeking out from under the knit gloves. I wondered if Carr could see it from across the room.

"I don't know," I said. My voice sounded strange, too high, trembling slightly. "They'd wonder why this man I baptized didn't go to church. Even if I didn't say anything, what if Michael tells them? They wouldn't like it."

Carr gestured emphatically with his huge hands. He pulled the hood back. A red glow, like a sunburn, had spread over his cheeks. "Then he can be your roommate. Utah Valley University's close to BYU. He can go there. You can help him get started."

I touched the bulging pocket on the front of the suitcase, tracing the raised outline of my friends' letters. Soon they'd be home from their missions. We'd planned to room together at BYU. In a steady back-and-forth over the last two years, we'd constructed a college life of long road trips and late night movies and pretty girls. Michael didn't figure into that plan.

"I have roommates," I said.

"But you can help," Carr said, his voice louder. "If you really think about it, you'll find a way. And then you'll take that paper out of the garbage."

We both looked at the open trash bag.

I was tired of pretending that I wanted to help Michael. "He's not the person I baptized." I pressed my open palm into the trash bag, hearing a puff of air and then the thin crackle of paper. "If he was still that person, it would be different. I'd help. But what he does now, I wouldn't even call him a Mormon. He's chosen a different life. He's not my responsibility." I stood and pulled the bag's orange drawstrings.

Suddenly, Carr was on his feet, moving quickly toward me. I stood to block him, but with a heavy swipe of his arm, he shoved me aside, and then he bent down, rooting through the clothes until he found the paper.

Something in me burst, and out came a hot flash of anger and revulsion for Carr I'd buried away every time I'd had to endure his habitual sluggishness and grating piousness.

I lunged for Carr's throat, but he swatted me away. I went down, my legs collapsing beneath me, my head knocking against the closet door. My eyes filled with tears, but I didn't know if I was crying or laughing at Carr. "Yes, take him home with you, " I said, as Carr retreated back to his bed, the paper cupped in his hands as if it were one of his fragile wire creations. "And what can you really do for him? You? You with all your good intentions."

Night had darkened the bedroom windows. My head throbbed. My arms and legs felt leaden. The floor seemed to quiver and jerk as I set my hands on the bed and stood up.

I carefully set the Gucci shoebox in my suitcase, next to the bootlegs. I didn't say anything to Carr that evening, or even the next morning as I lifted my luggage onto the express train for the mission home in Padova. I watched Carr from the train window. He sat on a wooden bench, a train schedule spread over his lap. His new companion would arrive in a few hours. I felt light and at ease, finally done with Carr.

The train lurched from the station and picked up speed, Ravenna receding into the green and gold countryside. I stared down at the cement ties of the adjoining track ticking hypnotically past. The train cut through a vast, rolling wheat field. I squinted. The wheat was a blinding, silvery white, shimmering and rippling in the breeze. For a moment, I experienced a dull guilt that radiated from my guts and washed up over my chest and shoulders. But when I touched the suitcase under my seat, the feeling subsided. Soon, I thought, one life would end and a new one—my life after the mission— would begin.

But in that new life, I soon came to know a persistent and troubling disappointment, even as the names of people and places, the finer details of that once consuming mission life, blurred and dimmed. With time, the Brioni ties, probably cheap knockoffs, lost their stitching and then completely unraveled. The bootlegs were unlistenable, static and boisterous crowds drowning out the music. And the Gucci loafers—somehow they were different from what I remembered buying, too effeminate, too elaborate and showy. "Oh no," my friends would shriek whenever I wore them, "Allred's got his fairy shoes on again."

Something from that time, though, seemingly impervious to decay, remains vivid and unforgettable: the image of Carr, like a sun-drenched still life, parked on that bench as the express pulled from the station, the open railroad schedule on his lap, his pudgy features—a face so calm and innocent turned in my direction but not seeing me. It was the same gaze I encountered years later one breezy April morning as I rounded a corner in downtown Salt Lake and saw Michael striding toward me. His unexpected presence stopped me cold. I wanted to hide my face until he passed—but there was no escape. Our eyes met. I braced for a scathing, venomous look, the hard set of a mouth and accusing eyes. But nothing. He was smiling, a bounce in his step, a man at peace with the world. He looked at me as Carr did so long ago from that wooden bench—as if he never knew me.

In That Classroom

In the fall of 2009 I got a job teaching math at Westside Alternative, an inner-city high school in Phoenix that didn't require any certification or formal experience, just a college degree. My parents were baffled. They couldn't understand why I didn't take a job with the engineering firm I'd interned for my last semester at Brigham Young University. But I wanted to do something altruistic, at least for a while, before I settled into life.

At the end of my first week at Westside, the school's founder and principal, a man named McCaren, called me to his office.

We sat across from each other, separated by a broad faux oak desk, bare except for a copy of my resumé and an orange Monster Energy drink that had marked the desktop with a half dozen wet circles.

McCaren leaned back. Something deep in the chair groaned as he shifted his weight. "Brigham Young University," he said. "BS in mechanical engineering, *magna cum laude*. An internship with HDR Engineering." He looked at me, starting at the thick soles of my brown Oxfords and moving up to the top of my head. "I want to put you on the school's homepage. A picture, a short bio." McCaren laid a large, freckled hand over my resumé. "I want parents to see this. Someone like you could boost our enrollment."

I felt a rush of heat rise through my shirt collar and into my cheeks. "Me?" I said. "I've never even taught before. I don't see how I can boost enrollment." But there was something I'd wanted to talk to McCaren about. A week into school and I wanted to do more. "What about an engineering club?" I asked. "I could be the advisor. Projects, field trips, competitions with other schools. Maybe that would help enrollment."

McCaren breathed a little chuckle that whistled through his nostrils. "I don't think most of these kids can even spell *engineering*. We have a hip-hop club and a dance club. That's what these kids like." He stared at me without saying anything, then looked down at my resumé. "You were a Mormon missionary. Where?"

"Los Angeles," I said. "Mostly the San Fernando Valley."

McCaren leaned forward, resting the dry knobs of his elbows on the desk. "All those dusty, blue-collar towns," he said. "Same kind of kids here, right? Marginalized, at-risk. You wanted to save them, didn't you? A mission. Isn't that the point?"

I wasn't quite sure what he was getting at. "I wanted to help them."

"You want to help these kids?" McCaren asked. "You want to save them? Get them through the door and into a seat. I hear you're doing great things in your classroom, but don't make it too hard. They'll bolt the minute it gets tough. We can't afford that. Sixty dollars per student per day. That's what the state pays us. No students, no *dinero*." McCaren lifted the Monster to his lips, not blinking, not taking his eyes from me, then set the can on my resumé. "This is triage, just the basics to get these kids into the working class. That's how you save them."

I nodded but didn't agree.

■■■

Daniel Garcia. He was in my sixth period algebra class, hair razored to his skull, sagging beige Dickies, a pressed white T-shirt that caught him just above the knees, a hard copy of at least half the male students at Westside. He'd emerged from the same brokenness and poverty as most of these kids—the absent father, the undocumented mom, an older brother who'd dropped out of school— yet he showed up every day, did his homework, got As. He'd scored in the ninetieth percentile on the state standardized math test.

After that first week of school, he started staying after class, and once the other students were gone, he'd tell me something he'd read about.

"You know, Cannon," he might say so quickly that he'd have to gulp for air between each sentence, "that NASA just found this habitable planet four light-years from earth. And did you know that life on earth might have come from Mars. Like maybe an asteroid knocked off some piece of Mars that came to earth with microbes on it." As we spoke, he'd cock his head toward the front of the classroom, his eyes bouncing between me and the open door.

He talked about wanting to build satellites for NASA or design missile defense systems. And the way he talked—it was more than a pipe dream, more substantive than the way his friends jawed about their ridiculous plans of dropping a rap album or walking on to the Phoenix Suns. And then Daniel's friends would show up at my classroom door and something would change on his face, a sudden air of indifference, not a care in the world beyond the moment. And then he'd leave.

What would happen to Daniel after graduation? As the months passed, the question took on greater urgency. There he was in his senior year, no college acceptance letter, no scholarship, no money squirreled away for even a semester at Phoenix Community College, no plan beyond high school. What could get him out of the inner city, away from his friends, toward college? A job?

But where? An internship? Doing what? I couldn't think of anything.

And then one night in January, as I sat in my apartment watching the evening news with its repeating loop of growing fatigue and national discontent for the wars in Iraq and Afghanistan, I had a thought that came to me suddenly. What about the military for Daniel? I had my own doubts about the war, its legality, financial costs, human rights violations; but the idea of Daniel enlisting seemed to have a sound logic. The drawdown had already begun. The president had committed to a complete withdrawal of American ground forces within a year. The war might be over before Daniel even finished boot camp. He'd probably be safer in the military than he'd ever be on Phoenix's Westside. And wasn't the military just what Daniel needed, what most of these kids needed, the routine, the discipline, the professional development, the boon of the G.I. Bill?

I wanted to bring all this up with Daniel, to step out of the easy back-and-forth of our brief afterschool conversations and speak with blunt candor about the world beyond Westside and his diminishing options if he kept his present course. But there was never time before his friends showed up, all giggles and grabassing, to lead him away.

■■■

Two weeks later I stayed after school to finish some lesson plans for the next day, long enough that it was dark when I walked to my car. I hadn't eaten since breakfast and my stomach growled with a raw, aching emptiness. I kept thinking about a taco truck not far from the school where I'd eaten a few times. That's what I wanted to fill the emptiness in my stomach.

As I squinted at the menu printed on the side of the truck, a thin body draped in baggy blue jeans and an oversize Phoenix Suns hoodie stood at the stainless steel counter in front of me, picking over a handful of change, a spattering of nickels and dimes in a mound of pennies. The woman who always took my order, gray-streaked hair pulled into a tight ponytail and coppery, sun-spotted cheeks, leaned through a narrow window above the counter, a single taco on a square of wax paper in her left hand. She gave me a nod of recognition and an apologetic smile. The thin body said, "*Lo siento*," a voice I immediately recognized as Daniel's.

I felt a sudden, heavy sadness press into me as I watched Daniel sift through the change in his hand.

I stepped to the counter. "Four more for him," I said to the woman. "And I'll take two *carne asada* and two *lengua*. And two Cokes. The *medio litro* in the bottle."

Daniel swung around. "Hey, Mr. Cannon," he said in a far-off, dreamy voice. He raised his handful of change and giggled. "I'm short a little."

I pulled out my wallet. "It's on me."

We sat at a collapsible card table in front of the taco truck, on flimsy plastic lawn chairs, and ate. A smell vented from Daniel's hoodie, something of skunk and pine strong enough to cut through the grilled meat and diced onions and cilantro on my plate. I could see it in Daniel's eyes, the raw red there.

He held a taco pinched between his thumb and index finger, hunched forward, shoulders rounded. He finished it in three quick bites, and then took another taco from his plate. "Where'd you get a taste for *lengua?*" he asked.

Traffic rushed by on 27th Avenue. I looked down at my plate but suddenly had no appetite. My left foot, as if counting time, beat a quick, nervous rhythm against the gritty asphalt. I kept waiting for Daniel's friends to appear, from behind the Dollar Store across the busy street, from the dirt alleyway on the other side of the taco truck, to call him away into the night. "Los Angeles," I said. "I was a Mormon missionary there."

Daniel's fingertips gleamed with a translucent layer of pork grease. "You ever try brain tacos, Cannon? *Cabeza.*" His cheeks bulged with meat and tortilla.

I wagged my finger. "That's where I draw the line. No brains, no *chiciornes,* no *tripa.*"

"You're talking about my comfort foods," Daniel said. "*Chiciornes, menudo.* My mom used to make scrambled eggs and cow brains for breakfast."

A blue Civic with tinted windows pulled into the parking lot, idling in front of the taco truck, bass thumping, muffler wheezing. I waited, expecting the windows to lower, expecting bloodshot eyes and dumb, grinning faces to emerge from the darkness, Daniel's friends calling to him. But the car pulled forward and then merged into the heavy traffic.

Daniel pointed at the moon. "You know there's probably water up there, in the shadows and underneath the ground. NASA thinks so. I just read about it."

I touched my bottle of Coke, felt its chill on my palm, heard the pop of tiny bubbles. "Where'd you read that?"

Daniel lifted a thin circle of radish and popped it in his mouth. "The library. I go Saturdays when my mom and brother work. Just me and the bums there."

I looked at the moon, and then back to Daniel. "So what happens after graduation? You hang out in the library every day? No college?"

"College?" Daniel rubbed his fingers together. "Got to have money."

"Last year, didn't the school counselor talk to you about college?" My voice ticked up a notch. "Applications? Scholarships? Financial aid?"

Daniel laughed, perhaps at my ignorance. "It's all about attendance, Cannon. That's all Westside cares about." Daniel rattled the change in the hoodie pocket. "Got to fill the seats to get that state money."

"It's a shitty school," I said, shocked at this admission. "Barely a school." I could hear something in my voice, something rushed and persistent and frustrated, and I knew Daniel could hear it, too. "But what about you, probably the smartest kid at Westside? Satellites, missile defense, the moon. How's that going to happen? Or do you just plan to read about interesting things?"

Daniel folded his arms across his chest and looked down at the table. "My brother wants me to go into business with him, mowing lawns. I thought I'd save for a couple years and then go to college."

"A couple years? A lot can change in a couple years," I said.

Across 27th Avenue a city bus pulled to the curb with a screech of metal and the hiss of air, disgorging its passengers, old men and women with plastic grocery bags twined around their wrists. "Two years," I said. "Three years, four years, five years."

Daniel looked up at me. I could see his anger. "What do I do, Cannon?" His hands had seized into fists. And then he pulled a handful of change from the pocket of his hoodie and let it spill onto the table. "This is it, all I got."

We stared at each other across the table. This was new territory, a place beyond the breezy back and forth of our afterschool conversations, more consequential and far-reaching.

"You join the military," I said. "You get out of Phoenix. You learn something. Satellites. Missile defense. Electronics. And then you go to college on Uncle Sam's dime."

Daniel nodded. "The military," he said, without surprise, as if he'd said the word a hundred times. "*Army Strong. Be All You Can Be.* They send me stuff, pens and key chains. They even call me. Staff Sergeant Ridge. They make you feel like the number one draft pick. My brother says it's slavery."

"The war's almost over," I said. "People are done with it. You enlist and spend your time stateside. Unless there's something better here?"

Daniel ran his hand over his shaved head, the short hairs bristling under his palm. The hood fell away.

The traffic rushed past. My question lingered in the silence between us.

▪■■▪

The day after graduation Daniel enlisted in the Army, though he said his mom and brother were against it. A week later he shipped out to Fort Benning, Georgia. I was proud of him. I thought I'd saved Daniel from Mc-Caren's and his family's status-quo narrative.

That summer and fall, we exchanged letters. He told me all about boot camp, the humidity, KP duty, PT at dawn, the hours of classes in marksmanship and orienteering, but recounted not with disdain but through the eyes of someone growing into a new life. He did well enough to be assigned to the Signal Corps for advanced training.

In February Daniel's unit deployed to Iraq, but he wasn't worried. The grunts coming back, he wrote, were bored off their asses. He'd be under ten feet of concrete in the Green Zone teaching Iraqi intelligence officers about satellite systems. But he said he wouldn't mind seeing some action, just a little, just enough to earn his Combat Action Badge.

And then it was early April, the Friday before spring break. I was nearly through my second year at Westside. I sat at my desk after school and graded midterms. It'd been a day of outbursts and distraction, students barely able to concentrate, their minds absorbed with the prospect of a week free from school. A steady electronic beat and the heavy smell of fried food drifted through my closed door, the hip-hop club continuing the day's merriment in the cafeteria down the hall.

I was tired, ready to toss the midterms in my bag and head home. The next morning, I planned to drive to my parents' house outside Seattle to spend the break. I still needed to pack. And then I heard a tapping at the door, so quiet I wondered if it was the music.

I walked to the door and opened it. Two men, not much older than some of my students, stood under the hallway's harsh fluorescent lighting, brown skin and thin mustaches, their eyes shadowed under black, sun-bleached baseball hats fading into the color of a dark plum.

One was short and thin, the physical opposite of his friend, who was taller and thick through the chest. Both wore long-sleeve, button-up shirts flecked with a dusting of dirt and grass. A whiff of gasoline and oil mingled with that of the frying food from the cafeteria.

"Cannon?" the shorter one asked.

"Yes." I didn't know them. I thought they might be part of the grounds crew McCaren had hired to mow the lawns and cut back the tall oleander that edged the front of the school.

"I'm Diego, Daniel's brother."

He spoke so softly, his head bent forward, his mouth pointed at the carpet, that I barely heard him above the music. I motioned them in and then closed the door.

It took a moment, but I remembered him from Westside's graduation ceremony in June, pulling at the collar of his blue-striped button-up shirt, shifting his weight from foot to foot as his mother, in a sleeveless yellow summer dress, a little unsteady in black high heels, fawned over Daniel, straightening the golden tassel on his cap and smoothing the front of his royal blue gown. "Daniel mentioned you," I said, walking back to my desk and easing into the chair. "He said you were at Westside a couple years back."

"Dropped out," Diego said. "Had to work." His voice had a nervous quiver. His eyes were red and watery under the bill of his hat. And then I remembered something that had bothered me, but which I'd forgotten until that moment: the way Diego had looked at me at graduation, the briefest of looks, how he'd scanned the faculty sitting on stage until our eyes locked. Something bitter and angry passed through his gaze.

I looked over at Diego's friend. He stood by the closed door, head turned away from me, as if he were listening for something. When I turned back to Diego, he was suddenly so close to my desk that I flinched. I could smell sweat and gasoline, dust and mowed grass.

"Have you thought about getting your diploma?" I said. "Westside has a free night school."

"Fuck this school," Diego said. "And fuck you." He pointed at me with a grease-smudged index finger, stabbing at the space between us. His lips curled back to show a row of clenched teeth. "You put it in his fucking head. Money for college. Honor. Discipline. I told him it was all bullshit. I told him to read some history, not what they give you in school. I kept asking him why he'd want to fight for a country that hates him."

I felt the tap of blood in my ears and an electric tingle in my fingertips. I raised my hands from the desk. "I'm not sure what you're getting at here." I looked at the classroom door. The friend stood there, now staring at me.

Diego's upper lip trembled. "They came last night in their uniforms, with their medals and their shiny shoes." The words came from deep in his throat, almost a growl. "Then they told us how he volunteered for some stupid patrol. And that's all they'd say. And this." Diego pulled a folded paper from his back pocket and held it in his fist. "You know how much? $100,000 for my brother's life. You think it's enough? Even for the poor?"

All at once, I saw the carnage of the evening news from the past seven years rise up fresh in my mind, thick, crumpled armor, cratered asphalt, oily smoke dimming the desert sun. "I'm sorry, I'm sorry." I heard the words, like a prayer, looping through my mind in a kind of distant reverb, and then I knew they were my words. I felt myself leaning forward in my chair, my elbows on the desk, my hands clasped together. I felt an unspeakable loss, felt a piercing guilt, but I suddenly understood why Diego had come to my classroom. The music pulsed through the door. I understood that no one would hear me. "I never forced him," I said. "I thought it would help pay for college. Please."

Diego brought his fists down on the desktop. A ceramic cup of sharpened pencils spilled onto the floor. "You didn't have anything to lose," Diego shouted. "You fucking *pinche pendejo*?" And then he broke into Spanish, the words raging out of him, too quickly for me to understand. But their meaning was clear.

Diego reached into his front pocket. Something in his hand caught the overhead lights. He flicked his wrist. Then I saw it, the black handle of a knife and a curved steel blade with a serrated edge. I stood up quickly, the chair shooting back and ricocheting off the metal chalk tray. In a moment like that you understand what a knife can do to your body.

▪▪▪▪

That classroom. There you are, so young, smiling, a teacher, only for a brief moment of your long life, and there they are down there, your students, asses parked in graffitied chairs, elbows on dingy desks—hungry, worried, scared, tired, barely able to keep their eyes open.

And for years after your time at Westside—in fact, for the rest of your privileged life—these are the thoughts that will haunt you in those small hours of the night as you consider who built that classroom, nail by nail and stick by stick:

Eleventh grade, your winning long jump at a track meet that sent you to regionals, a half-inch farther than Atticus Gacoki, a Kenyan immigrant from another school, and how the man holding the measuring tape looked at you and winked, a sly smile, like a secret, creasing his pale, whiskered face.

You'll remember your grandfather, a retired civil engineer for the City of Idaho Falls, a former leader in your church, a bishop, a counselor in the stake presidency, how one summer day you rode with him in his new Lexus SUV, heading across town to hit a bucket of balls at Sand Creek Golf Course, when two Black men in a cream-colored Escalade pulled up next to you at a stop light, enraged that your grandfather had cut them off, and how the driver leaned out the window and called him a cracker motherfucker. And then, before taking a quick right and speeding away, the man spat a wad of yellow phlegm that splattered the top of the windshield. And your grandfather, a deep red sprouting through the collar of his blue Calloway golf shirt, saying in a voice you hardly recognized: "They're all over town now." And then he looked at you, as if he were about to share a secret. "Fifty years ago," he said, "we would have stuck a fork in those niggers and turned them over."

And you, a few years later, in your starched white shirt and black missionary tag, teaching a young, undocumented couple from El Salvador about God's plan of happiness, and you, practically euphoric with what your mission president preached that morning at a training meeting. "Elders and sisters," he said, gripping the sides of the pulpit, his eyes misty. "As God's faithful servants, you have more power and authority than any worldly king or queen." You looked at the man and woman, at their worn clothes, at their tan, round faces, at the slight decay on the edges of their front teeth. How you wanted to save them!

But on that Friday before spring break, in that classroom, a knife pointed at your guts, you can only process a single thought: how the world, once so safe, is now rife with danger.

▪■■■▪

Call it luck, call it coincidence, call it divine intervention, call it nothing, but as I stood by my desk and pleaded with Diego, the fire alarm above the door suddenly blared a deafening screech that filled the room. Diego winced and brought his hands to his ears. The classroom door flew open. McCaren was there with Dan Wilson, the P.E teacher and football coach. White smoke swirled above the fluorescent lights in the hallway and drifted into the classroom.

McCaren rushed in, waving his arms. He pushed Diego's friend toward the door. "Out," he yelled. "Out, out. There's a fire in the kitchen."

I bolted from the room and down the hallway with McCaren at my side. I looked back and saw Diego standing in the classroom doorway. His face was blank, no hint of surprise at this interruption to whatever plan he'd had—as if this were just another injustice he couldn't fix.

Outside, I hurried to my car, pausing only for a moment to look at a pickup truck parked next to me, a blistered, brown Toyota whose bed sagged with the weight of a lawnmower, a weed eater, and a blue tarp bulging with mesquite branches.

And then I drove to my apartment, a gated complex in north Mesa with a lush, landscaped courtyard and a swimming pool surrounded by palm trees. I wanted to feel safe. But I couldn't sit still, couldn't help tensing when I heard footsteps shuffle past my front door, couldn't help peering through the thin slats of the blinds if a snatch of conversation carried up from the courtyard. Later that night, I couldn't sleep, a guilt churning in me, wanting out, yet I felt something even more immediate and urgent: a primitive desire for self-preservation in a world I suddenly couldn't control.

And as I drove north the next morning through vast, isolated regions, scanning the rearview mirror, scanning the parking lots of rest areas, that crippling sense of menace eased as the sun set and the arid land gave way to the forested mountains of western Washington, country roads, and finally to the narrow gravel lane where I grew up.

"We ordered Chinese food," my mom said as I stood in our living room. The windows were dark, and only the TV illuminated the room with an eerie white light.

"How's life in the trenches?" my dad asked. He was sunk deep into his plush La-Z-Boy, his face reflecting the electric white of the TV. A plate heaped with food rested on his round belly. He squinted at the TV. A man's giant head floated there above a black and white banner that said: *Can Iraq Defend Itself?*

"War," I said.

I eased onto the couch, suddenly so exhausted. I nodded off, but not fully. I could hear the mechanical rat-tat-tat of machine guns, the scrape of tank tracks, and the fuzzy drawl of American voices on radios, all of it a background to the man's rabid voice that pitched higher and higher.

I heard Daniel's name. My eyes snapped open. There, spread across the TV screen, I saw a picture of Daniel. He stood next to an American flag, in a beret and a black formal jacket with stamped brass buttons, the corners of his mouth curled into the faintest suggestion of a grin. A banner running across the bottom of the screen said: *U.S. Troop Killed in IED Attack Outside Baghdad.* I felt on the edge of something, ready to bury my face in my hands and weep.

I looked at my parents, waiting for them to acknowledge this lost life, a hand to the mouth, a mournful shake of the head, a word or phrase about the poor family. I wanted an entrance to unburden myself, to free this sadness and guilt. But my parents didn't even notice Daniel, didn't even look at the TV screen. They were in the middle of a petty argument, my dad complaining about the Egg Foo Young on his plate and the measly portions, and my mom telling him that if he cared so much, he should have chosen the restaurant.

I stood, unnoticed, and walked outside. A full moon floated on the horizon. The air had the warm touch of spring, but a chill drifted up from the damp lawn, like a cold breath on my face and bare arms.

▪■■▪

Monday morning I called McCaren and told him I wouldn't return.

"What you're feeling," he said, his voice barely more than a whisper, as if he were at my side, his mouth close to my ear. "God, I can't even imagine. One of your students. Some kid you tried to help." I heard the crackle of tiny bubbles and a rush of liquid. I could imagine the sweaty can, the pink tip of a tongue sliding over freckled lips. "But don't you want to pull some good out of this? For these kids. Don't you want to save them?" His breathing quickened. "We'll put his picture in the lobby. We'll make a little garden memorial with a plaque. These kids need a hero. Hell, why not name the school after him? Parents will love it. He's a patriot—"

I hung up.

That night at dinner, I told my parents I was done teaching. They looked at each other across the bucket of fried chicken in the center of the table. Something passed between them, as if this were the end to a private conversation about me that had started long ago. They seemed relieved. "Don't feel bad," my mom said, dabbing the corners of her mouth with a napkin. "I'm sure you did a lot of good. They were lucky to have you that long." My dad held a drumstick to his mouth. "A high school teacher with an engineering degree." He shook his head. "That equation never made sense to me."

But what I never told my parents, or anyone, was how the next morning I drove to the Army Recruit Station in Federal Way to put my name to paper to enlist as a private in the United States Army. I imagined a grand gesture to calm my guilt: stepping from that classroom, stepping from a privileged history, standing shoulder to shoulder with Daniel and Diego, with all of my students. And as I drove, I wanted to believe that's what I'd do, as quiet country roads turned into crowded highways and then into wide, congested city streets, even as I sat in front of the recruiting station and watched in its streaked windows the warped reflection of a strip mall and a gated apartment complex.

A cold wind pushed a torn plastic grocery bag past the station's glass double doors as a low, dark cloud began to shed a spray of fine droplets over the windshield. The car was warm, the seat comfortable, and the city beyond the rain-flecked windows only a soft, distant hum. I never went inside.

The Water Between Us

for Jen

Lately when I call her at work, she's taken to firing off questions, like she's in the habit of keeping pace with the ringing phones and hurried conversations around her. With all those questions, she winds pretty easy. Just the realities of pregnancy, I guess. But maybe it's more than that. Now she's all business at work, all efficiency, nothing wasted. No chitchat. Just the facts.

She says, "You hear back yet on those jobs, Spencer?"

I say, "Not a word. Bad time to be out of work, Anne."

She says, "And that company on Auburn Way?"

I say, "Talked to them this morning. Truthfully, I think they're tired of hearing from me."

I'm calling her from home, dressed and work boots on but nowhere to go. Just me and the TV—but no news cycle. I can't take it, all that talk of bankruptcy and bailouts and unemployment rates. Makes me feel like a statistic. Instead, I got this infomercial on. The Ronco Rotisserie Oven. Ron in a green apron and a pink collared shirt, hefting a roasted chicken for the audience, who can't seem to get enough, grinning and shaking their heads in stupid disbelief. A man in an apron and a pink shirt, holding a roasted chicken—and that smile. I guess when you own the company, when it's your show, you can smile like that, apron and all.

Anne says, "And what about that place on C Street? What's the name? Work Today, Paid Today, right? It'd get you out of the house."

Ron slides an entire pork roast into a rotisserie oven. A dozen rotisserie ovens, loaded with hot dogs, bratwurst, racks of ribs, and stuffed chicken breast, whirl behind him. Work Today, Paid Today. I close my eyes. How do I tell Anne? How do I describe that dim waiting room, the scuffed floor and grimy lawn chairs, the sour smell of worry and fear? How do I explain all those sad, hungry faces? There's no time. She's too busy.

I say, "Anne, I'm telling you. Nothing."

I hear her fingers tapping at a keyboard. A phone rings twice, then stops.

She says, "Something will come along." But the words sound empty. Her mind is elsewhere, I can tell, her eyes fixed to a screen, puzzling out, just as she'll do most nights at the kitchen table long after I've gone to bed, all the rows of numbers, the circles portioned into colored slices, the thin columns rising and falling—a language I can't make sense of.

I say, "It's in the cards, Anne," and maybe I hear the same emptiness in my voice. I touch the remote. Ron and the grinning audience and the rows of spinning rotisserie ovens vanish, and there's only a screen, shiny and black as a piece of obsidian. I have to stand up. I have to move. I have to get out of the house, out of this quiet that seems to press in when Anne's not there, and lately even when she is. In this house, I'm beginning to feel as heavy and lifeless as the furniture. I tell Anne, "How about we meet up at Game Farm Park? Noon?"

The phone pressed to my ear, I can almost see Anne in her cubicle, the computer, the open calendar, the scroll of the mouse, the quick glance at her watch, her mind ticking through a half dozen small calculations, all the unavoidable adjustments to meet me. "Sure," she says, "okay. But I have a meeting at one." Then a quick sigh. "I have to go, Spencer. My manager wants to meet."

▪■▪■▪

Four years ago, when we were just married, I was at Sandberg Construction in Algona, same job I worked for a year after graduating from Auburn High, same job I came back to after two years as a Mormon missionary in Lubbock, Texas. In all that time at Sandberg, I'd worked my way up from a shovel to an excavator. I'd learned enough to take pasture, nothing but field grass and blackberry thickets, and put in sewer and drainage, grade it, measure out sidewalks and streets, then lay asphalt and pour concrete.

Back then I'd say, "This is temporary, Anne, just until I save enough money for some equipment and a piece of land. I won't have to work for anyone. My own company. My own crew."

She'd say, "I like ambition."

She was finishing up at Green River College and waitressing nights at Mitzel's. Sometimes I'd stop in after work, steam rising off my damp Carhartt jacket. I'd squeeze into one of the padded booths, and then we'd pretend we didn't know each other, like it was a game. She'd hand me a menu and fill my glass with water.

I'd say, "What do you recommend? The salmon? The steak?"

She'd say, "Sir, for you the salmon."

I'd say, "No. The steak. Rare."

I'd wink and run my hand down her thigh if she was close enough, give her breast a squeeze when she'd lean over to fill my glass.

She'd say, "Sir!"

I'd say, "Pardon me, Ma'am."

After all day up to my knees in water and muck, digging trenches and laying pipe, I thought I deserved her attention. It seemed the proper order of things. A day's work and a hot meal. Someday there'd be a house on a nice piece of land, a covered place for my equipment, a big workshop, a company I'd call my own, and a bunch of kids running around. I'd give Anne the life I thought she deserved.

Then last November Sandberg dies, right there in his pick-up on the 167. Heart attack. His wife sold everything, gave the crew a little bonus, cried a lot and told us how sorry she was.

That was right before the housing market bottomed out. Banks stopped lending. No building. No hiring. The Great Recession, they're calling it. And that's where I'm at, not a prospect in sight.

But Anne's moving forward. She finished her Associates and transferred all those credits into a business management major at UW Tacoma. Now she works in marketing for a biotech firm in north Auburn, some Singapore company unaffected by the economic dip. I should be happy for her, and I am, for the work she's put in, and grateful for what she's making, more than I ever did. She talks about wanting to be Director of Marketing, maybe a VP down the road.

But after ten months without work, I got nothing, just a dozen resumés in the wind. And all this time at home I've been thinking about when Anne worked at Mitzel's. I don't know why, but I can't shake the image of me sitting there in that damn Carhartt jacket and those muddy Danner boots, watching Anne weave through the tables with a pitcher of water in each hand. It's like she's moving toward something, real slow but moving. And then I see myself there in that booth, touching her thigh as she fills my glass, and I think, "He has no right. None at all."

▪■■▪

This is just a low moment in life's ebb and flow, I guess, or at least my parents keep telling me that in one way or another, on the phone, when they drop by or invite us to dinner on Sundays. They say life is just such that it's hard getting a footing at first, that it's all part of the Lord's plan that will eventually reveal itself. They say it's in God's hands, on God's time, but I wonder if they blame Anne, like her work has thrown our lives onto a different path than the one they took. Ever since she landed this job, I sense a change in how they see her, like how suddenly this girl from Buckley, the waitress and community college student they first knew when we got married, has become someone else, jumped from one world and up into another.

Now my mom's taken to calling me every week, thinking I'm depressed, and maybe she's right, in that way moms know things, like they're tuned in to some deeper level. At some point, the conversation always comes to Anne and the baby, and my mom says something like how she's sure Anne can't wait to quit and stay home with the baby.

What do I say? I thought having a kid would reset things to how we planned our life when we got married, back to the way we'd been taught and raised at church and at home, those Primary songs we sang, that life of a man returning home each night to find his wife and kids there, all smiles and hugs. I thought having a kid would be the leap of faith God needed to open a door somewhere for me, even if it meant pulling up stakes for a while and moving the family to Colorado or North Dakota where some guys I knew from Sandberg were in the oil fields waiting out the recession. And now after all these months at home, with all that time, I can't stop thinking in a way I never did when I had work. Anne quitting her job, giving it all up to stay home? When I think about it, this strange thought keeps circling back, this idea of Anne and me as identical paper cutouts, same height, same shape, so no one could pick out man or woman.

"Maybe I'll stay home with the baby," I told my mom when she called last week. The words surprised me, and I wondered in what dusty corner of my mind that thought was sitting in. I had to laugh, like it was a joke, just to cut through what those words really meant. But in the silence between me and my mom, I marveled at the words, turning them over and over like I would some interesting rock pulled from a dirt pile.

My mom sucked in a mouthful of air. "You stay home? Spencer, that's just not the way things should be. What would your father say?" And in that I heard how my parents see Anne, like now she's some weird kind of other. I heard suspicion, a questioning of faith. But it's aimed square at me too, all the pep talks over the last ten months without work, a gentle nudge about the kind of man I was raised to be, the provider and protector. Those paper cutouts of Anne and me—there's that thought circling back again. What if one of those cutouts has a good job and the other no job at all? Faith or no faith, you can't feed a family dreams. They don't pay a mortgage.

■■■

I pull into Game Farm Park, and there's Anne, hair tied back, standing next to a play area with swings and plastic rocks. Her navy blue cardigan gapes just enough to show a round belly pushing at her white blouse. Her head's tipped to the sky, eyes shut, the sun catching her full in the face, a scene I almost don't want to disturb by putting myself into it. Sycamores rise around her, dropping yellow leaves onto the grass and empty parking lot. It's the end of September, a warm, cloudless day before rain, a day in high school I'd have sluffed off after lunch to throw a line in the Green River for nothing more than to watch the sun hit the water.

"It's so quiet," Anne whispers as I step from my truck. She puts a finger to her lips, then points to the sky. "The leaves. You can hear them falling through the trees."

All I hear is the tick of the cooling engine, but I can taste the air in the back of my throat, the rot of leaves and grass in the heat, summer's last legs, and for a moment I'm lightheaded.

Anne takes my hand. "Let's walk," she says. "Doctor's orders." And we move slowly along the sidewalk, past empty tennis courts and soccer fields, and then onto a narrow strip of crumbling, weathered cement running along a mossy levee above the White River. We stop at a bend where deep water hits shallow rocks.

"Rushing water," Anne says. "The sound always reminds me of something I read in an English class, something like water and meditation are forever wed. Maybe it was Melville. I don't remember. You ever think of water like that?"

With the toe of my boot, I nudge a chunk of the crumbling walkway over the bank. It tumbles down to the water's edge, a jagged lump among the smooth river rocks. Water. I think of an early morning, pole in my hand, a long cast as the sun just lights the sky, the current against my legs. But I can't hold the thought. Instead, something gloomy creeps in. All I can think about is water boiling up when I'd dig down to lay sewer pipe, seeping in where I don't want it. I know water's rot in summer heat, its sting on a cold day. But I don't tell Anne that. Her cheeks are red, her eyes fixed to a distant spot beyond the alders and sycamores on the other side of the river. Her breath comes quickly from the walk. She's happy and content, in the grip of something I don't want to upset.

She turns to me, a little smile bending her lips. "So this morning my manager wanted to meet, out of the blue. I was nervous. I kept wondering if I'd messed up. But it was actually really good news. She said the company's starting this program to pay tuition for employees who want to go back to school. She said if I want to move up, if I'm serious about it, I should think about an MBA. She said the University of Washington has a weekend MBA program I should consider. I told her I'd really think about it. Of course, after the baby. Maybe next year."

Her words come at me with the force of rushing water. I can barely hear, barely think. I look at Anne, pale and beautiful, but I can almost picture her dissolving until she's no longer there. But then this other thought: that maybe I'm dissolving, all that water wearing me away until I'm nothing. I breathe in, so deep my throat aches, like a breath might keep me next to Anne a little longer. "Is that what you want?" I ask.

"It's an opportunity. It's stability." Anne slides her hands into the pockets of her cardigan. "Maybe in a couple years, with my job, we could buy a house in Lakeland Hills or Heather Highlands. No more renting." She takes a hand from her pocket, like she's not even thinking about it, and touches the top of her belly.

Stability. The word. A little shiver in my guts rises into my belly and churns there. Then it washes up over me, across my chest and onto my shoulders, the weight of something like hopelessness. This life we're living, Anne with her work, me at home with nothing—it suddenly seems like it's all led up to the very spot we're standing on. "And that life we talked about when we got married?" I ask.

Anne doesn't say anything, and for a moment there's just the sound of water between us. "I don't know," she says quietly, almost in a whisper, like a confession. "Maybe it's changed. I know your parents don't get it. My dad doesn't, either. But my mom—maybe she does, but she wouldn't admit it. I keep thinking that there's the life we talked about, the life we're expected to live, then there's the life we have to live."

"But that life we talked about," I say. "We can still have it." I want Anne to see, I want her to believe, even if just for a moment. And I want to believe, too. "When the economy picks up, when people start building again, I'll have work. And a company someday."

"Someday can be a long time," Anne says. "Or someday can be never. My dad always talked about someday." She shakes her head and laughs, an easy laugh, but with a dark, raw edge to it. "He was always swinging for the fences with some business idea that never worked out. There were so many. Flipping cars. Rent-to-own cars. Detailing cars. Always cars. What he should have done is go back to school. That's what my mom told him. Our bishop, too. Everyone at church. Instead, it was always just one more big idea."

"That's not me," I say. "We won't have that life, all the scrimping and saving."

Anne looks out at the river. "I keep thinking about my mom, staying home all those years, all she had to do: Food on the table, clothes for us, which bills to pay each month to keep the lights on. She was so tired, I remember, barely able to keep her eyes open most nights, but she always helped me with my math homework. Algebra, geometry, trigonometry. She was a wiz. You know what she told me once, out of the blue, the two of us at the kitchen table working on a quadratic equation or something? How she'd wanted to study civil engineering in college.

She only mentioned it once, and then never again, like she was ashamed of it. And what happened? No college. Marriage and kids. And years later, with the kids gone, what does she do? She's a receptionist in an engineering firm, answering phones, cleaning up messes in the break room. I can't stop thinking about that, Spencer. I wonder: every time she sees all those blue prints, the bridges and the buildings, does she think, 'Those could have been mine.'"

Anne looks down. My hand's on her elbow, though I can't remember reaching for her. It's like somebody else's hand there. I let go quickly, like I've been caught at something, then I stare downriver to where it bends into the trees, and only then can I look at Anne again. A watery layer pools in her eyes, and I see the fading green of the sycamores and the silver of the river reflected there.

"But it's not just money," she says, a little catch in her voice. "It's like for years I was a nobody in so many bad jobs, all to become somebody in a job I really like. But giving that up to stay home, just having that one identity. I don't know. It doesn't seem fair."

How can I argue with that? It's that word *home*, what it means, all the good and the bad stuffed into it. Maybe I know some of the bad now, maybe in a way I never have, home as a place where the dry tick of the clock and the churn of the dishwasher barely cut through the silence, a place where the walls can close in, but where the windows look out on a world where everyone else seems to live a better life than mine.

"And me?" I say. "What do I do? I'm stuck."

Anne takes my hand. "No, you follow your dream. You build your company."

"And our kids?" I ask.

"They'll be all right," Anne says. "We'll make sure of it."

The river churns below us, the water splitting around dark boulders. In the shallows, I catch a flash of black and silver, then a slick, gray fin and a tail that break the surface, a Chinook salmon pushing upriver to spawn. It holds close to the bank, suspended there before vanishing into the dark water. In two weeks, the river will be alive with them.

"I have to go," Anne says, wiping at her eyes.

She takes my hand and we walk back along the broken walkway to the parking lot. I feel the thrill of Anne's words, a company of my own, a crew, projects lined up, all with her blessing. I feel light on my feet, the heavy darkness gone from me. I breathe deep and take it all in, the river, the trees above, the path before us spotted with shadow and sun, and I can't help smile as a vision of another, better life rises up in my mind: Anne in a bright, windowed corner office; me on a job site leaning over a thick stack of construction plans, my crew, my equipment in motion around me; our kids, with their friends, cross-legged on a carpeted floor, pressing Legos together; and our home, a looming thing with an arched entryway, hardwood floors, and granite countertops. *Our home.* The words move through my mind, flick on my tongue. It's all I can think about as I kiss Anne goodbye and drive down Auburn Way. *Our home.* I say it, over and over, this fantasy of what our lives can be. *Home.* I say it like it's a spell that will bring that life to us.

The Righteous Road

My mom cupped her hand over the phone. "It's Reed," she whispered.

I wished she hadn't answered. I took the phone from her and leaned against the countertop. "Hello," I said. "Hello."

"What, Derrick? No call?" Reed asked.

"I didn't know you were home." I lied.

In November Reed had sent a practically illegible postcard. He was always sending postcards, from Istanbul, Mumbai, Munich, Hong Kong, all written in a sharp, hurried scrawl. *Let's get together over Christmas*, he'd written. *It'll be like old times.* I'd studied the postcard: a crowded open market in Jerusalem, bins of dried fruit and lentils, skinless goat and lamb carcasses suspended from steel hooks.

And then there were his letters, as long as novellas, self-aggrandizing rants stuffed in manila envelopes he'd decorated with intricate and baffling designs. His message was always the same: the minute details of his service among the impoverished and downtrodden masses, and his grandiose plans for a future that had us saving the world from tyranny and environmental annihilation. I couldn't finish the letters, nor could I respond with equal enthusiasm. The letters were too didactic, trying to persuade me to recapture some embellished past. Unlike Reed, I'd grown up, moved on, gone to college. I was in my last year of law school at Brigham Young University. I was engaged.

"I knew you wouldn't get my postcard," Reed said. "They were going through my mail. *Mossad*. Israeli secret service. Sometimes they'd follow me. " He said this as if the inconvenience of wiretaps and surveillance were a fact of his workaday world. "What's important is that you're here," Reed said. "There's someone who needs our help. Eight at my house. You in?"

I could only guess who this somebody might be: the Palestinians, Mexican border crossers, old growth Douglas firs, the spotted owl, hump-backed whales? I imagined one of Reed's windy, vainglorious speeches, a call to action to save the oppressed or right some ecological wrong, and me sitting there nodding ecstatically—as if I were still a devotee of the cause. I was ready to tell Reed I had to catch a plane in the morning, which was true. I was flying to Salt Lake to spend the weekend in

Park City with my fiancée, Cassie, and her family. But the thought of another night playing Scrabble with my parents while my dad grumbled about his irritable bowels and diminishing retirement seemed unbearable. Worse, I imagined Reed showing up at our door.

"I'll be there," I said.

My mom was on me the second I hung up. Behind her, the Christmas tree winked on and off in a way that hurt my eyes.

"I've always felt something was off with Reed," she said, "even when you were little boys. And all that mischief in high school. I never believed you thought of it yourself. His parents had a handful. Edna Swenson still calls me. She cries about him. Did you know that? She wonders where she and Bob went wrong. She blames herself."

"Boys will be boys." I said this to get a rise from her, not because I believed it. I was of the opinion, and had been for years, that Reed needed to move beyond the perpetual adolescence he lived in.

"But when do boys grow up?" my mom said. She began rearranging the nativity on the coffee table. "You grew up. Maybe you can talk some sense into him." She pointed a wooden shepherd at me. "Tell him to go to college and stop giving his parents grief. Tell him to go back to church. He's still young enough to serve a mission. It's Edna's dream."

"I'm not going to talk some sense into him," I said. I didn't want the responsibility of steering Reed back into the fold. Besides, Reed worshiped Mother Earth. His congregation convened in the tops of trees while angry loggers cursed from below, or outside third-world sweatshops where the oppressed toiled for a nickel an hour. His sacrament was a thick joint and cheap wine.

"You just be careful over there," my mom said. "I can't imagine he's changed much. Still the same old Reed."

Her concern annoyed me—as if Reed had any influence on me. He was a vestige from another life, an adolescent, idealistic incarnation of myself I would never revive.

▪■■▪

We grew up in the same wooded subdivision outside Auburn, Washington, had the same teachers at Lake View Elementary, attended the same ward. The sandbox, Sunday school, Cub Scouts, T-ball. When didn't I know Reed?

He always had this deeper ecological and humanitarian consciousness. Our Sunday school teachers, sweet old ladies who brought us oatmeal cookies, stared incredulously as Reed decried the cruelty of Mosaic animal sacrifice or questioned the goodness of a God who required the massacre of every Canaanite living in the Promised Land. At twelve, Reed's first youth talk in sacrament meeting was a five-minute rebuke of God's command to Adam and Eve to subdue the earth and have dominion over it. "Why can't all His creations just have an equal relationship?" Reed pled from the pulpit, his voice quivering with emotion. "Why can't everything just be free and happy without people messing up the forests and the air?"

When we were fifteen, Reed's ecological sense found a focus. It was one of those boring summer nights, nothing to do but sit in Reed's living room and flip through channels until we were catatonic. The only thing on was a paid Greenpeace advertisement soliciting donations to protest the Icelandic seal hunts. I watched in horror as a man in a blue, fur-lined parka clubbed a pod of yelping harp seals to death. The saliva drained from my mouth and a nauseating weight bloomed in my lower guts. I wanted to turn the channel and forget this injustice, find a brainless comedy to purge the image of the doomed seals. Reed made a choking sound. His lower lip trembled. Snot oozed from both nostrils. I pretended not to notice.

And then in the middle of all that slaughter, the deathblows and the skinned seal carcasses, the camera shifted to four men dragging a Greenpeace activist across the blood-spattered ice. Tall, with a blond beard and fierce blue eyes, the activist chanted something about stopping the slaughter. He was Lars Norgard, we later learned, captain of the *Sea Shepherd*, a man of mythical proportions who'd made a name for himself over the years by ramming a dozen whaling ships.

Wiping the snot from his nose, Reed said, as if in a trance, "That's what I want to be."

Reed called a toll-free number that flashed on the TV screen, and in a couple weeks some brochures came in the mail. We pored over each color photograph: the *Sea Shepherd* slicing through the glacial, turbulent North Atlantic; hippy kids chaining themselves to the bows of fishing boats; and Lars Norgard, with his thick blond beard, standing on the *Sea Shepherd's* bridge, barking commands into a CB as he stared down a Russian whaling ship. What more could two fifteen-year-old boys want? Adventure, danger, heroes and villains, the open seas. We wrote Lars and volunteered our services. We'd do anything: scrub toilets, cook food, wash laundry, whatever he needed.

Lars actually wrote back. We sniffed the envelope and thought we could smell the briny sea. While applauding our commitment, Lars said by law we'd have to wait until we were eighteen. Until then, if we really wanted to stop the bastards, we should send money for fuel. "Keep believing and continue the fight," he wrote. "Patience. When the time comes, I'll have two spots on the *Sea Shepherd* for my eco-warriors." The words thrilled us.

We must have gotten on a mailing list. The pamphlets and newsletters filled Reed's mailbox: Animal Liberation Front, Amnesty International, PETA, Doctors without Borders, the Sierra Club. Shocked and sickened, we stared at the sharp color images of clear-cut wastelands and veal calves wallowing in their own feces, at skeletal Somalians with distended bellies. Before, such abject suffering and unchecked destruction had only existed in the abstract, a brief image on the evening news. My parents had shielded me, I knew, and now I wanted to do something about all this misery and devastation, something more than praying for the sick or cleaning out flower vases at Mountain View Cemetery for church service projects. All that seemed ridiculously inconsequential when I considered the dying whales and the vanquished ancient forests and the starving Somalians.

When we could finally drive, we skipped school one Friday to check out an animal experimentation protest Reed had seen advertised in the *Seattle Weekly*. There were about a hundred people there, chanting, waving signs, and marching in front of a towering glass and steel skyscraper in downtown Bellevue. One protester, in a fluffy rabbit suit splashed with red paint, writhed on the sidewalk. Another wore a dog costume and had Vaseline smeared over his eyes. He howled as a woman led him around by the paw. Truthfully, Reed and I thought it was a bit much, until we looked at the literature a protester handed us and saw the lab photos of terrified beagles hanging from their paws, the kittens with electrodes protruding from their skulls, and a chimpanzee running on a caged treadmill. All that suffering so Meyer Chemical could sell us lip balm and antifungal cream. The protesters' outrage was contagious. Reed and I walked up to a short, middle-aged man in dreadlocks who seemed in charge and asked if we could help. Smiling and then giving us both a bro hug, he handed us signs. For the rest of the afternoon we marched, blocked sidewalk traffic, and upbraided anyone who dared enter the building.

After that, we were sneaking up to Seattle a couple times a month to march and pass out literature at anti-fur rallies or to knock on doors for Amnesty International. At night, we'd head out with other activists to spray paint butcher shops and furriers with pithy slogans like *Feed it, don't eat it* or *Are clothes to kill for?* Afterwards, we'd hang out in some grimy apartment in the University District or near Capitol Hill to listen to rousing tales of environmental and humanitarian adventures while Phish and the Grateful Dead played in the background and a joint and a jug of wine passed from hand to hand. We partook because these were the fruits of the earth, or so they told us, a shared sacrament for nature's children meant to enlighten the mind and strengthen the body. If I experienced any guilt after that first toke, these assurances certainly mitigated it, as did my budding awareness that as an only child I felt controlled and smothered. I wanted an identity apart from Mormonism and my parents' conservative politics. My parents bored me. No hobbies, no friends they went out with, no interest in music and art. If that was righteousness, I didn't want it.

Soon, Reed and I stopped eating meat and dairy. We refused to wear our black leather church shoes, refused to wear any brand that exploited its workers in third-world sweatshops.

At home, my parents said little about my activism, probably believing it would pass. Reed, however, felt morally compelled to win his sister and parents over to his way of thinking. He saw the roots of their ecological and humanitarian apathy in what he called the naïve and narrow-minded strictures of Mormonism. Suddenly, Reed's rhetoric burned with anti-religious sentiments: religion as a social construct, as a mental illness, as the opium of the people. He could go on for hours, until I couldn't take it anymore. His home became a den of acrimony, screaming and vague threats from Reed's parents, a constant tension simmering just below the surface. Soon, Reed refused to attend church and early morning seminary. This appealed to me, too, for no other reason than that I longed for more sleep. My parents, probably sensing Reed's influence, offered unrestricted use of my dad's old Plymouth Reliant and a Shell gas card if I didn't miss a day of church or seminary. Even Reed liked the idea. Without a car, how would we get to Seattle?

And then in January of our senior year, Reed didn't show up for school on Monday. At lunch, I called his house. No one answered. When I got home that afternoon, my parents sat solemnly on the living room couch. My mom dabbed at her red, weepy eyes with a crumpled Kleenex. My dad, who shouldn't have been home for another two hours, stood and pointed to the love seat. "Derrick, we need to talk," he said. My heart pounded.

He said Sister Swenson had called that morning. Reed and two activist friends had been arrested in Seattle Sunday afternoon for vandalizing an Albertsons meat counter. But there was more. Brother and Sister Swenson, distraught and suspicious after receiving this news, had gone through Reed's drawers and discovered a joint and a bag of mushrooms. "Do you know anything about those?" my dad asked. "Are you and Reed using drugs?"

Staring at our beige carpet, I denied everything, denied vehemently while suddenly realizing my parents knew. I was sure.

Reed was now on a plane to New Mexico, my dad said, where he'd spend the next twelve weeks in a wilderness treatment program for drug addiction and behavioral issues. He insisted, at least while Reed was gone, that I take a break from the activism and from our little cadre of hippie friends at school. Now I'd eat lunch with the kids from church. Did I understand? My dad wanted to know. Or did he need to go upstairs and rummage through my drawers and closet? I stared at his polished black Wingtips and nodded quickly.

The next day at school, the church kids—all bores and blind followers of the faith, Reed and I thought—invited me to eat lunch with them, an invitation arranged, I was sure, by my dad and Bishop McKinley. I accepted their invitation, hoping it might allay some of my parents' suspicions. And I'll admit, after two years of fiercely debating the environmental or humanitarian issue *du jour* over lunch with Reed and our friends, I actually enjoyed the cheery, inconsequential conversations about church dances, BYU football, and future mission calls. I sat with them for a month, though I never told Reed.

∎∎∎

Reed's first postcard came two weeks after his abrupt departure. "Living off the fat of the land," he wrote. "Stars so pretty. Grateful to the Creator for all good things. Searching for a heart at peace." A week later another postcard: "At harmony with the world. Love and respect for all people." He'd included an enigmatic postscript, a quote from Edward Abbey's *The Monkey Wrench Gang*, a book we'd both read at least three times. The postscript said: "Because we like the taste of freedom, comrades. Because we like the smell of danger."

It wasn't a surprise, then, at least to me, when Reed escaped.

After a search of the area around the camp yielded no Reed, the sheriff's department got involved, blazing out into the high desert on motorcycles and ATVs, even in a helicopter flown up from Albuquerque. Search and rescue volunteers came from Santa Fe. With no sign of Reed after three days, his parents flew to New Mexico. The ward fasted and prayed for Reed's safe return. My parents, I'm sure assuming Reed was dead, asked if I'd like to talk to a therapist. Not necessary, I told them, believing Reed was out there immersed in his wilderness dream, holed up somewhere, living off the fat of the land. But as the days passed, I considered the possibility that Reed might be gone. At night, unable to sleep, I found myself kneeling at my bedside, something I hadn't done in a long time, praying for my friend's safe return. I somehow knew, with an assurance I couldn't articulate, more a feeling than anything else, that Reed was all right.

And then a week later he called his parents from Pueblo, Colorado. Incredibly, Reed had endured the freezing, high-desert night and walked fifty miles to the interstate, then hitchhiked 350 miles to Pueblo. He was staying with some guy who was president of the local clean air conservation group.

Reed's parents flew to Pueblo and pleaded with him to finish the treatment program. He refused. He wanted to go home. His parents wouldn't hear of it. Reed had strained the family to the point of rupture. They quickly reached a compromise with Reed, one that showed their desperation. Until the end of the school year, they'd rent a studio apartment for Reed near the high school, pay his utilities, and give him a food allowance. He could come home once a week for Sunday dinner. Not a bad arrangement, Reed thought.

Every day after school we smoked weed there, and Reed would often lay out his vision of our lives after graduation, how we'd travel the world over in search of perilous humanitarian and ecological causes to throw ourselves into. It was talk, or so I thought, the idealistic machinations of a young man on the cusp of the adult world. Realistically, the next year I saw us at Green River Community College, done with the weed and the booze, hitting the books. And then at nineteen, I'd always assumed Reed and I would do what had been ingrained in us from birth by cheery primary songs and a thousand talks and Sunday school lessons. The mission. I'd meant to bring it up with Reed: the mission as an altruistic adventure, two years serving the indigent gentry of some third-world backwater, learning their language, teaching them to love one another. What was wrong with that? I also understood the unspoken stigma of not going.

Though I hadn't told Reed, I was tired of the Seattle activists and their scene. Loud, pushy, self-righteousness, they disliked almost everything and would go on endlessly about anarchy and environmental destruction as if they knew nothing else. Ragged clothes and bad teeth, many looked indistinguishable from the homeless begging dollars at freeway off ramps and downtown intersections. I didn't want the ascetic's life, nor did I aspire for excess and luxury either. I wanted a few comforts, a life equal to or a little better than my parents'. A decent home for my family. Maybe a nice car. Nothing wrong with that.

But if anything, Reed was becoming more radical, more dedicated to the cause. He had other plans for us.

It was a Friday at the end of May, two weeks to graduation, when he waved a hand-written letter in my face and said, "You want out of this hole? Here's your ticket." We were at his apartment, smoking a joint. Kurt Cobain screamed from the stereo. I squinted at the letter through a haze of smoke.

"Freedom and adventure. Saving the world," Reed said. "Right? Everything we've talked about for the last three years."

Reed, always audacious, always sniffing out the next adventure, had written Lars Norgard to remind him of his promise, and then, to prove we were ready for a life of activism, he'd detailed our activities over the last three years. Lars wrote back. We were in luck. There were two spots on the *Sea Shepherd*, but we'd have to act quickly. He'd be docked at the Tacoma Marina for a couple hours on Monday, June 13th. And then Lars warned us that this was the most dangerous work in the world and how he couldn't guarantee our safety. Reed read those words, smiled, and then read them again.

I feigned excitement for the next two weeks as we bought rucksacks from the army surplus store in Seattle and stuffed them with everything Lars said we needed: wool pants and sweaters, rain gear, lug-soled boots, waders, sunscreen. I smiled as we concocted our plan to meet that Monday morning at the bus stop behind JCPenney. I'd park the Reliant on Main Street, leave a note for our parents on the driver's seat, and then we'd take the bus to Tacoma. I praised the soundness of the plan, knowing that I never intended to meet Reed.

That Monday, the day after our high school graduation, I lay in bed and listened to the phone ring and ring and then go to the answering machine. I was alone, my dad at work, my mom at a church quilting project. "Where are you?" Reed's voice boomed through the house. "Derrick!" He called again and again. I heard him through the pillow I'd put over my head. Finally, I picked up the phone. I felt that I owed Reed at least that.

"You sleep in?" he shouted. "Are you sick?"

I cleared my throat. "I'm not sure . . ." I struggled to finish the sentence. "That life. I'm not sure I want that life." I tried to explain: the transient, hand-to-mouth existence, the pessimism and never-ending activism. "What about college?" I asked Reed. "And missions. I thought after all this we'd go on missions."

"Missions?" Reed said. He seemed confused. "Why would we go on missions?" And then he drew in a sharp breath. "You believe," he said slowly. "You believe everything they taught us."

I believed, believed weakly, perhaps believed through association only, a subconscious absorption of faith as I slept through church and early morning seminary. I believed, maybe because my parents believed, because despite all their buttoned-up, conservative stuffiness they'd loved me unconditionally. I imagined that God, if anything, might be an extension of them. I wondered if the church would even let me go on a mission, after all the weed and the alcohol and the vandalism done in the name of saving the planet. I'd have to make amends. Tell my parents everything. Meet with Bishop McKinley.

"I won't even get into how ridiculous it all is," Reed said. I could hear the disgust in his voice. "Angels and gold plates. But that's not even the worse part. It's the culture, Derrick. The Mormon factory. You go on that mission and you walk straight in, and when you come out, you're just like them. You dress like them and think like them and talk like them. You live in your little bubble. You see that, Derrick? Is that what you want?"

"But what if we do it differently?" I said. The idea came to me suddenly. I held the phone tightly to my ear and paced the living room. "Not like our parents. What if we did it our way and still believed?"

"Do it differently?" Reed said. "It's not in the program, Derrick. They don't want that."

I heard the hiss of air breaks and then the monotone crackle of a voice over a speaker.

"Derrick," Reed said. "Come on. There's still time. You don't think we can do some good? There's other ways to do good."

I felt a rawness in the back of my throat. "I'm sorry," I said.

That night I called Reed's dad. There was no anger or accusations. Brother Swenson thanked me, and that was it. Reed was eighteen. What could he do? I knew the truth. He was glad Reed was gone.

I spent the year at Green River Community College, attended the stake singles' ward, made restitution and repented for what I'd done. I received a mission call to serve in Rio de Janeiro. After those two years, I enrolled at BYU and earned a degree in political science. And then law school. I hadn't seen Reed in seven years, but in that time, a month had never passed without a letter or postcard from him.

▪■▪■▪

At eight, I stood on Reed's parent's doorstep. Loud Arabic music rattled the windows, strings and a high androgynous voice locked in a repetitive groove. I knocked hard and waited.

The music stopped, and then a moment later Reed stood in the doorway, smiling. He wore a Greenpeace T-shirt, faded jeans, and a white knitted beanie. "Seven years," he said, taking my arm and pulling me into the house. "Seven years and look at you now: the lawyer in embryo. You gonna stick it to those fat cats in their corporate towers?"

"Sure," I said. I could only imagine the selfless narrative Reed had conjured up for me, the rabid environmental lawyer saving the world from greedy land developers and wicked industrialists intent on melting the ice caps and decimating every forest. Actually, I was leaning toward corporate law. My dad agreed. The hours were long, but the money was good. The previous two summers I'd clerked in Latham and Watkin's Los Angeles office, and I was optimistic they'd offer me a job after law school. I wanted stability. I wanted to provide a comfortable life for my family. But I knew my aspirations would mean nothing to Reed. He'd think there was no adventure in it, nothing of the bravado and altruism we'd dreamed about and discussed years ago while smoking a joint in his apartment. Worse, he'd think I'd become one of them, sold out for the all-powerful dollar.

"And you, the world traveler," I said, because I knew that's what Reed wanted, a little opening to gush about his adventures, to sing his environmental consciousness and deep empathy for others.

"I've been a few places," he said, ushering me toward the couch. "But it's good to be home, right? The old stomping ground. You want something to eat or drink?" he asked. "Some juice or cookies?"

"No, I actually just ate."

He insisted. "Come on. What can I get you?"

"Really, I'm fine," I said.

"You have to try this tamarind nectar I brought back from Gaza," Reed said.

He was halfway to the kitchen before I could protest.

"How are you parents?" I asked, hoping they'd materialize from somewhere. I was uncomfortable around Reed. After so many years, he felt like a stranger.

"Still preaching their conservative conspiracy theories," Reed shouted from the kitchen. "Still pining for Reagan and the Cold War. God help us all. Actually, they took my sister and her husband to Crystal Mountain for the night. They're sick of me already."

Reed returned with a plate of baklava and two glasses brimming with an opaque liquid. He handed me a glass and then set the plate on the coffee table. He took a long drink from his glass, smacking his lips and looking at me expectantly. The liquid had the sheen of motor oil and smelled slightly fermented. I took a sip and cringed as the sweetness hit my fillings.

"Good?" Reed asked, before emptying his glass.

"It's different," I said, taking another sip. I looked around the living room, at the beige carpet and the black leather La-Z-Boy. Nothing had changed in ten years. In fact, I was sitting on the same brown microfiber sectional where we'd first seen Lars Norgard protesting the seal hunts. "How's Lars Norgard?" I asked. "What's he like?"

"A phony," Reed said quickly and unequivocally. He picked at something under his thumbnail. "'Fuel to help us get the bastards,' my ass. The man's a gambling addict. And"—Reed knocked his knuckles together—"he's a carnivore. An environmental phony. I was done with him a long time ago."

"Well, it's good to see you," I said. "Really good." I tried to think of more to say, to dredge up some nugget from years ago to carry the conversation, some innocuous memory we could bat around for a minute. I asked about Israel.

"Palestine," Reed said. "The Zionist propaganda wants to erase history, like no one lived there before 1948. Gaza and the West Bank are concentration camps. Genocide. People dying every day, and no one hears about it. I wanted to change that."

I was confused, but not surprised. "I thought you were studying Arabic. Didn't you mention that in a letter?"

"Just a cover," Reed said. He put his hand over his mouth and laughed. "My ticket into the country. A lowly student at Berzeit University. My mom was thrilled. I didn't tell her that I was a human shield. And then the

Zionist pricks caught wind of what I was doing. Israeli Secret Service. They think I'm an insurgent. Can you believe that?"

"A human shield?" I said. I thought of longhaired, wild-eyed hippies throwing themselves in front of bulldozers. "Don't people die doing that?" I could only imagine the swollen image Reed had of himself: the solitary, undeterred student halting that massive tank in Tiananmen Square, the revolutionary, a savior to the oppressed.

"It happens," Reed said stoically. "It's war and war has its martyrs. 'Put your bodies upon the gears and upon the wheels, upon the levers, upon all the apparatus.' Mario Savio." Reed shoved a piece of baklava in his mouth. "At Ramallah and Nablus we stopped the Israelis. We built roadblocks. But that's not all. Remember how I always said I wanted to fight in a revolution?"

Reed was on a roll now, warming to the subject. When he reached for another chunk of baklava, I glanced at my watch. I thought of letting him go on for another fifteen minutes before I made my exit.

"None of that passive-aggressive shit," Reed said. "I wanted the real thing. Tear gas and Molotov cocktails. I knew these guys in *Hamas* and sometimes I'd go out with them at night. Patrol, they called it. What a rush. I even got something to show for it." He inched up his sleeve to show me a gauze bandage wrapped tightly around his bicep, and then he unwound it with a practiced dalliance. As the gauze fell away, I saw a crusted red gash about an inch long. "The kid standing next to me got it in the stomach," Reed said. "I don't think he made it."

"Someone shot you?" I was incredulous.

"An Israeli sniper." Reed cradled his arm as if it were a badge of honor. "Revolution, brother, the real thing," he said. "Twelve-year-old kids blowing themselves to pieces on Israeli buses. They're committed. You have to admire that."

Reed stood and walked into the kitchen, raising his voice so I could hear. "Oppression. That's what it is. People should never be oppressed." He returned with a full glass of tamarind nectar. "Bullies," he went on, staring down at the glass as if reading something on its dark surface. He walked to the window. "Isn't the world full of them, from the playground to the corporate office to the White House? Aren't they everywhere?"

"Everywhere," I said, not in agreement or denial, but merely because that's what Reed wanted to hear. His breath came in short bursts. I looked at my watch and wondered if my parents were in bed yet.

Reed paced the room, passing the glass from one hand to the other. "When I was in Venice last summer, I ran into Liz Schuller at a bar near San Marco's Square. What were the chances, right? You remember Liz from high school? Carly Cantwell was her best friend. You remember Carly. Your little crush."

"Carly Cantwell," I said, her name strange on my tongue. We'd had some classes together our junior and senior years. We'd even studied together a few times.

She was a shy girl, a state champion swimmer with curly blond hair and a lean body tempered from long hours cutting through water. I had a crush on her, sure, one of those pubescent musings that never comes to anything. She wanted to be a doctor, I remembered. I wondered about her sometimes when searching my bookcase and seeing the green and gold binding of my high school yearbook. "Did Liz mention Carly?" I asked.

"Oh, yeah, buddy, she mentioned Carly," Reed said. "In fact, I think she told me a little more than she wanted to. *In vino veritas*, if you know what I mean."

"What'd she say?" I tried to sound casual, but I suddenly found it difficult to breathe. I wondered if something had happened to Carly.

Reed stopped his pacing and looked at me. "You really want to know? You ready for this? Denny Bradshaw raped her the summer after our senior year. It happened at a house party. He cornered her in a bedroom. Sure, she tried to fight him off tooth and nail, but Denny's huge. And in the middle of it some girl walks in and then just turns around and leaves. Doesn't do a damn thing. Carly's crying for help and the girl bolts."

I stared at my hands. They suddenly felt cold. "Did she tell the police?" I asked. I wanted to hear that justice had been done, that Denny had been punished, though I already knew the answer.

Reed sat on the coffee table and leaned in toward me. "You see, that's the kicker, my friend. Right as Denny's zipping up, he tells Carly he'll kill her if she ever tells.

She's in shock for about a week before Liz convinces her to file a police report. But the police won't do a thing. That's the legal system for you. They'll give you all the justice you want unless it interferes with what Big Daddy Bradshaw's passing under the table."

Denny Bradshaw was a grade above us, a high school athlete. His father sat on the school board and owned the largest construction company in Auburn. I remembered Denny as the arrogant athlete with his shoulder lowered, pushing through the school hallways as if moving down the field, shouting at anyone in his way. At least once a week at lunch he'd stop at our table with a couple jock friends to wave a hamburger in our faces and laugh hysterically. Once he overturned a garbage can on top of our heads. After high school, he went to Washington State University on a football scholarship, but only lasted a couple years before dropping out and moving back to Auburn to work in the family business. I'd heard a rumor that his father cut him off for embezzling money.

"And you know the girl who walks in the room," Reed said, "the only witness who can put Denny away? She's a secretary at Bradshaw Construction. Started a few weeks later. A real coincidence. And what about all the other victims. Liz said there were always rumors."

I looked down at my fisted hands. "It's not right," I said.

"Of course it's not right. It's a tragedy." Reed walked to the window and frowned at the darkness beyond the glass. "And with guys like Denny the great injustice is that it keeps happening. I'd bet my life on it. Seven years after high school, you think he's changed? The man's a predator and we're going to stop him."

Reed turned and stared at me, as if expecting me to say something.

"What? You want to blindside him in an alley?" I asked. "Sneak up behind him with a crowbar? Is that what you're suggesting?"

"Hell no," Reed said. "I'd never harm a living thing. That's not what I do. I want to shame him. I was thinking about a little body work on his car, leave a message he'll understand, let him know somebody's watching."

"Reed, come on." I tried to laugh. "This is crazy. Really."

"I've done some reconnaissance," Reed said. "He works at that old bar on Main Street. The Mecca. He parks in the back. One or two minutes. In and out. We'll leave him a nice note."

"I'm in law school," I said. "We get caught and I'm ruined. I couldn't take the bar."

"Is that all you care about now?" Reed asked. "Come on. If we don't do it, then who will?"

"It just doesn't feel right," I said.

Reed laughed. "Doesn't feel right? Isn't there a higher law? The spirit of the law? Don't you believe that? And what about everything we used to believe in? Making the world a better place. Helping those who can't help themselves. Don't you believe that anymore?" Reed ran his thumb over the short stubble on his chin. "Okay, think about it this way: what about that rapist running wild out there?" Reed pointed to the darkened window, as if Denny were out in the backyard at that very moment, lurking in the bushes. "Does that feel right? What about some justice for Carly? Doesn't she deserve it?" When I didn't say anything, Reed kept talking. "Don't you see this shit every day on the news? The Denny Bradshaws of the world pushing their way through life, knocking people to the ground, mouthing off, wanting a free ride? Don't you remember how he'd push us around? And let me ask you this. Didn't it piss you off that we couldn't do a thing about it? But what if we could? Tell me, Derrick, and be honest, how would it feel to stick it to Denny? To send him a message?"

I didn't say anything, just stared at my hands, but I knew it would be wonderful, sheer bliss.

"You want to do what's right by the law," Reed said. "I respect that. I value that. But I'm going."

▪■■▪

Two weeks later Reed called me in Provo.

"The team's back together," he said, "fighting injustice. Just like old times." His voice sounded as if it were percolating up from the bottom of the ocean. "Hey, I'm in El Salvador until June and then it's off to Honduras. Maybe you've already heard about the exploitation down here, about the sweatshops. Nike, Reebok, Gap. We're talking 19th-century England, children working their fingers to nubs for a dollar a day. So how about it?"

I felt the weight of the phone on my shoulder, and then the heat building between my ear and the molded plastic.

"Correct me if I'm wrong," Reed said, "but maybe you're not interested."

I moved the phone to my other ear.

"I hope," Reed continued, "that you don't hold something against me."

"No, it's not that." And then I thought: *It's what you are and what I am now. I don't want to be you. I can't be you.* I remembered Denny's car, not the souped-up muscle car I'd expected, but a beige station wagon, clean and well maintained, the kind of car my dad would buy. A small photograph hung from the rearview mirror. A woman in a white dress holding a baby, and behind her lush trees and lawn.

There was a momentary roar on the other end of the line—a passing truck or bus. I imagined the tropical heat, the crowds of perspiring bodies, the chatter of a language I didn't understand, the smell of rot and food permeating the streets.

"Derrick, I know what you're thinking," Reed said. "You're thinking, 'He made me do it. He made me smash that car. The sinner made me sin.' Have you become one of them, Derrick? You gonna say your prayers tonight and write your tithing check and feel so wonderful because your God will right every wrong in the life to come? If you believe that then you're a bigger sinner than I am."

I unplugged the phone and walked to my bedroom. It was snowing outside, white flakes collecting on the bare branches and dead, yellow lawns. A car passed. The apartment was silent, my roommate gone, shopping or studying in the law library.

From the closet's top shelf I took down a cardboard box full of Reed's letters. Each envelope was decorated with a dizzying arrangement of intricate designs: arabesques, paisleys, loopy-loops twisting and falling in on themselves in a practically untraceable pattern. I saw in the elaborate patterns a complex network rooting back through the years, back to someone I didn't want to be or think about, back to Reed.

For the next half hour I fed the letters into the shredder under my desk and listened to the high-pitched whine as the paper disappeared into the machine. I found myself repeating something I'd once read, perhaps something I'd taught in Rio's crumbling *favelas*. *To rid our lives of sin, we must destroy its roots.*

·■■■·

I never imagined Reed living a long life. He didn't either. In high school, he enjoyed mulling over the possible scenarios of his passing. They were all heroic and horribly violent: pulverized by an explosive harpoon while protecting whales in the northern Atlantic; hacked to pieces by a crazed band of militants as they overran a Red Cross hospital in Sudan; ground to pulp and hair under the wheels of a logging truck. For Reed, anything less would have been unworthy of his life, and so he had lived, always searching out that dangerous, altruistic cause to throw himself into.

So when I answered the phone one Saturday morning and heard my dad's voice—strained, fighting for composure—I knew what he'd say.

"Bob and Edna Swenson called this morning," he said. "It's Reed. He's dead."

I stood in the living room and watched Cassie at the kitchen table, laptop open, searching online for the best stroller and crib money could buy. We'd been married about a year and owned a house in Burbank's Magnolia Park. I was an associate in Latham and Watkin's Los Angeles office.

My dad said the American Embassy in Honduras didn't tell Bob and Edna much, just that Reed was there with a group protesting the treatment of workers at a textile mill outside Tegucigalpa: picket lines, boycotts, even sabotage of some of the looms. The Honduran police didn't know if Reed's death and the protests were connected, but they found him, stabbed three times in the chest, a block from his hostel, pockets emptied, shoes stolen.

"Do they know anything else?" I asked.

"His knuckles were bruised," my dad said. "He didn't go down easily." And that's what I wanted to hear, that Reed went out fighting.

And then my dad said: "Bob and Edna asked if you'd speak at the funeral. Will you do that? It would mean a lot to them."

Outside, birds sang in our lemon tree. Down the street someone gunned an engine. "Sure," I said. "If that's what they want."

I hung up the phone and then walked over to the window. Parked in the driveway, my silver BMW glowed in the mid-morning sun. Cassie's yellow Tea roses and Santa Barbara Daisies edged the front yard. Later, our gardeners, Miguel and Hector, would come to cut the lawn and hedge the bushes. Like my pioneer ancestors, I'd prospered, cultivated my garden, sanctified materialism. I'd served an honorable mission, pursued education, found gainful employment, married in the temple, paid a generous tithe, would soon be a father. I was the elders quorum president. I should have felt like a success.

"Who was that?" Cassie asked.

I turned to look at her. I could already see the small bump pushing at her waistline. "My dad," I said. "Somebody I knew from high school died. He called to tell me."

"A friend?" Cassie asked.

I lifted my laptop and walked to the couch. I'd never told Cassie about Reed, never mentioned our years in high school, nor did my parents. There was something unspoken with my parents, as if we'd agreed that those years never happened. There were other things I didn't tell Cassie. I didn't tell her that twice a year I donated to Earth First! and Amnesty International. I didn't tell her that I had opinions I didn't share with our church friends.

"Just someone I knew," I said. "My parents want me at the funeral, as a favor to the family."

"Are you all right?" Cassie asked.

"I'm fine," I said. "We weren't close."

I needed to buy a plane ticket, pack a bag. In a couple days, I'd be home, sleeping in my old bed, eating my mom's food. And then the funeral, the bright chapel and drab organ music, and of course Reed, laid out in a dark suit and white shirt, hair trimmed—finally the missionary his mother had dreamed of. I'd stand at the pulpit and say something kind and comforting, something about Reed's love for all living things. But I couldn't say everything. Looking out at all those devout, grieving people who believed Reed's life was a tragedy, how could I say that maybe he'd died a brave man, a rich man, a righteous man?

The Private Investigator

The doorbell rang as I hung up the phone, and then I heard my father's deep, imposing voice fill our entryway.

I stood and walked slowly into the unlit hallway, unnoticed as my wife, Allison, hugged my father and then took his coat and bag. Though she'd only met him once, at my mom's funeral, I wanted her to share my dislike for the man. From what I'd told her, Allison knew enough about him to warrant a little enmity, or so I thought, but she cheerfully chatted away, asking him about the traffic through Primm Valley and the weather on Cajon Pass.

I heard my father's voice but hardly recognized him. His face was lean and bony, and his hair, thin on the top of his head, had gone almost completely white.

I stepped into the entryway.

"Hey, Champ. How you doing, Slugger?" he said, calling me the pet names of my childhood. The jarring unexpectedness of those names seemed to burst in my ears with multiple frequencies, bringing vividly to my mind twilight summer breezes and the metallic peal of ball connecting with bat under the insect buzz of stadium lights—the sounds of another time, nostalgic and melancholy and irretrievable. When I didn't say anything, my father gazed over my shoulder into the living room. I stepped aside to give him an unobstructed view: the black and white family photos of Allison and me against a weathered brick wall in Old Pasadena, our sons Henry and Jake slack and smiling in our arms; the Tuscan leather sectional and the hand-knotted rugs; potted palms in the corners of the room and English ivy draping the built-in mahogany bookcases. I wanted my father to see all of it. I wanted him to take in each soft, smooth surface reflecting the warm, rich glow of the life I'd given my family.

"Beautiful home," he said. "Magnolia Park. My favorite stretch of Burbank. I guess the P.I. business is all right. Must keep you busy."

"Too busy," Allison said. "You'd think Troy's a long-haul truck driver with how much he works. And then last month he was called to be the bishop. At least now he has to be nice to everyone."

"A bishop?" My father squared his shoulders so he stood a little straighter. His fingers fluttered against his pant legs. "Your mom would be proud." He turned to Allison: "And my grandsons?"

"In bed," Allison said. "They're rascals at the dinner table. Trust me. We wouldn't have a minute of peace. But they'll be up early. You can surprise them. All week I told them grandpa's coming."

I stared at my father. A stranger passing through or a man trying to make an impression? I wasn't sure. He wore tapered kakis with crisp pleats, tasseled Gucci loafers, and a loud Tommy Bahama polo shirt blooming with red and yellow hibiscus flowers. The pendant lamp above us flickered on the glass face of the silver Omega chronograph strapped to his wrist. My mind buzzed with the incongruous arithmetic of what I knew about his personal finances and the cost of the watch and the loafers.

I knew about his life, more than I'd told Allison. It was at my fingertips: bank records and credit reports, a spotty work history as an entry-level sales rep with a half dozen companies, two short-lived marriages after my mom, some bad checks in Montana that almost landed him in jail, and a DUI outside Reno. I even had his home address. No charming bungalow on a tree-lined street, no bougainvillea-draped arbor or broad, shaded porch. The Google street view of his North Las Vegas apartment complex brought to my mind the crumbling stucco, dark stairwells, and disintegrating jalopies of the blighted fringes of the San Fernando Valley where my investigators and I often staked out fraudulent insurance claims and delinquent debtors. The bare, inglorious reality of my father's life comforted me. I was glad to see how low he'd fallen.

"Let's eat," Allison said, nodding in my direction, as if to prompt me. I realized I hadn't said a word since my father's arrival.

I lifted an arm, an awkward, wooden gesture, to direct him to the dining room, but instead he laid his right hand on my shoulder. "Give the old man a hug," he said. I almost stepped back, as if his embrace were a punishment. But I stopped, barely flinching as his hand drummed against my back. When he let me go, I looked closely at his face, at the spotted skin stretched tight over the cheekbones, as if the skeleton were working itself through. I could smell him, the rankness of age mixed with a sharp, citrusy cologne. I hadn't seen or spoken to him in four years, not since my mom's funeral, where he'd shown up late, uninvited, and then slouched in a side pew with a bored expression on his flushed face, seemingly more interested in the clock on the chapel wall than in what was said about the woman who'd once been his wife for fourteen years. His conspicuous boredom and the alcohol on his breath had infuriated me, and I let him know it. We'd argued after in the cemetery parking lot. But in those four years, my father had become an old man, slightly stooped, dappled on his face and hands.

He stared back at me with an air of uncertainty and hesitancy, perhaps wondering where we stood, what I knew, what I'd forgiven.

"Yes, let's eat," I said, walking into the dining room, my father trailing behind me.

■■■

My father stood over the table, sniffing the air like an animal on a scent. "You've gone through too much trouble," he told Allison, giving her a courtly bow before sitting down. She pooh-poohed that idea as she stuck a serving spoon into a steaming bowl of mashed potatoes. "We're glad you're here," she said.

As we ate, I watched my father. He barely touched his food, just pushed it around his plate. I knew I was searching for something in his cadence, in his words, a gesture or facial tic. What was I looking for? Maybe a flicker of guilt and remorse. Just their fleeting shadows would have satisfied me. But I saw nothing of them as his initial unease seemed to melt into a cloying braggadocio, my father as I remembered him, a gravity pulling all the attention in a room to himself. He sat slightly reclined, one elbow parked regally on the armrest, his dreamy gaze fixed on some point behind us, a king on his throne with a captive audience.

He jabbered on through dinner about his adventures as a traveling sales rep, his stellar sales record that had garnered him awards and honors, the stars and world luminaries he'd happened to bump into on his sales trips, their big-hearted invitations to visit them in Beverly Hills and the Hamptons, and, of course, the dangers of traveling desolate roads where he'd had to defend him self with his trusty Smith & Wesson .38. In retirement, he planned to go abroad to live like a king in Bolivia or Ecuador.

Allison listened with an enthusiasm I couldn't muster, leaning in toward my father, clucking her tongue and shaking her head, encouraging him with spirited interjections like "Oh, that's incredible!" and "No, he said that!" as if she were gossiping with a neighbor over the back fence. She seemed taken in by my father, but all I could hear was the silver-tongued phoniness. He spoke as if he were living the high life, a revered and well-compensated employee, a magnetic soul people clamored to befriend. Of course, there was no mention of the spotty work history and the dumpy Vegas apartment, the failed marriages and the bad checks.

"So what about you?" my father finally asked me. "How's business?"

I crushed the linen napkin on my lap and noticed, for the first time, how the glass bowl holding the mashed potatoes was shaped like a rose. The idea seemed ridiculous.

My father appeared to read something in my gaze, an incredulity and irritation pushing through the neutral expression I'd tried to project since his arrival. His eyes dropped to his plate, where he busied himself cutting a green bean into sections. He suddenly seemed winded, the unease of earlier a palpable presence between us.

When I didn't answer, Allison said, "Troy, tell your dad about that car accident outside your office. I want his opinion."

My father looked up expectantly, fork poised above his plate.

"You tell him," I said.

Allison stared at me, her lips pressed together, and then she turned to my father:

"There was a bad car accident outside Troy's office," she said. "A FedEx truck ran a red light and T-boned a Latino guy in an old truck full of yard equipment. You know what Troy did? He grabs a camera and starts taking pictures of the accident. And then he gives his card to the man, who by that time's laid out on a stretcher in a neck brace, all banged up. You know what happened? Just yesterday he calls Troy, barely able to speak English, to say he's suing FedEx and wants to buy the pictures. Five hundred dollars. That's what Troy charged him. I told Troy he should've just given him the pictures for free."

My father slapped the tabletop with his open palm. "Way to sniff out a buck," he said. "Just like your old man. Carpe diem. Make hay while the sun shines." He patted Allison's hand, as if to reassure her of something. "FedEx will settle for two hundred times what the guy paid for the pictures. He could buy five new trucks with the settlement. He could go back to Mexico and live like royalty." Then my father leaned back and crossed his arms. The story reminded him of something that happened to him when he was younger, and then he was off again on a string of self-congratulatory tales.

I couldn't listen anymore. I couldn't even look at him, at the way his whole body shook and then collapsed with laughter, as if he'd been struck by something funny. I suddenly felt constricted, the chair narrowing against my hips, the table boxing me in, my thick sweater holding me like a straight jacket. A thin sweat glazed my nose and forehead. I wanted to claw at the sweater, rise and throw the chair back, run from the dry, heated air in the dining room and escape into the night.

"I have to leave," I said, standing so quickly my chair almost toppled over.

"Troy!" Allison said. Her fork fell through her fingers and clattered across the wood floor.

"Earlier. That was Eric on the phone," I said. "He can't do surveillance tonight. He's sick."

Allison stared at me. "Can't this wait? I mean, why do you have to go?"

"This is a big case," I said. "There's a deadline. It's priority."

"Can't someone else go?" Allison pressed both her palms onto the tabletop. "You own the company. Can't you get on the phone and make someone else do it?"

"It's too late," I said. "This is my responsibility. It's important."

"There are other things you're responsible for," Allison said, her head tilting in my father's direction.

"A doctor's divorcing his wife because she's a drug addict," I said. "Unless we prove that, she gets custody of the kids. Think of the children." I looked at my father. I wanted to see his face, the absorption of what I said. "I'm sorry," I said. "I have to go."

My father flashed me an easy smile. "My son, the private investigator," he said. "Don't worry about us, Slugger. You go out there and get her."

I pulled my camera from the hall closet, then opened the front door. Dark, heavy clouds filled the sky like a great expanse of upended mountains, each sagging peak like a tightly clenched fist. The tennis courts across the street in Verdugo Park were as brightly lit as a stage. A man and a floppy-haired teenage boy, obviously the man's son, grinned and stared up at the gloomy sky between volleys.

"When are you coming home?" Allison asked.

"I don't know," I said. "Late."

·■·■·

I drove north on Scott Road, squinting up at the Verdugo Mountains, but they were more shadow than substance, lost to the night and to the looming storm, except for a faraway red light on Tongva Peak that pulsed like a heartbeat.

I thought of Allison and my father at the dining room table, and how my father, this man I hardly knew, would soon occupy a bedroom down the hall from mine.

He'd quickly become a stranger to me after leaving, a belated birthday card with no personal addendum to the printed words; the occasional postcard scratched with a nondescript sentence or two I could barely decipher; a phantom my mom scrimped and saved to take to court for a meager check that might or might not come by the fifth of the month. He was like a person I once knew, a distant presence distilled down to a handful of contradictory memories—though the sound of his voice, strangely, had never diminished in my mind, its deepness and resonance, reading me the Hardy Boys, or describing in tantalizing detail, as we tossed a baseball in the backyard of the home we rented in La Crescenta, the life he planned for us, the turreted mansion on Point Dume, the yacht and private jet. It was this voice, my mom later told me, so confident and sure of its power to persuade, like something on TV, that had charmed her when they first met, my father, a lapsed, half-hearted Mormon who appeared one Sunday in her Las Vegas singles ward, and who, like her, had lost both parents at a young age.

His was a voice, I was to learn, that acted as collateral for the most fabulous promises and claims, to my mom, to the gullible strangers my father would unabashedly seek out in parks and restaurants, and to the naïve members in our La Crescenta ward, impressionable newlyweds and middle-aged couples ill prepared for retirement. He had a knack for sniffing out the insolvent. With that voice he could lull people into spilling their financial guts, then he'd shake his head and say something incredible like, "I bet you want to quit that rotten job" or "I know a way to pay off that mortgage in ten years," as if he'd long ago liberated himself from such workaday matters.

Later, some of them would sit in our living room, and I, as my father insisted, was to be at his side, smiling and nodding, a picture of unwavering filial confidence and trust, as he described an ironclad investment or a wave-of-the-future product certain to bring wealth and prosperity: vacation rentals, magnetic shoe inserts, a patented gas additive to radically improve fuel economy—of course, all for the price of a start-up kit and a cut of whatever they sold to their friends and family. The Armani suit he wore for these occasions and the BMW that magically appeared in our driveway the day of these meetings fortified my father's grand promises and claims. His impassioned promises of wealth and leisure, the vagueness of his products, the evasive, half-answered questions—only years later did I recognize my father as a fraud.

The hokey side businesses never paid out. His day job, something with real estate, something nebulous and suspect, never paid out, either. Not long before he left, I remember three silent Latinos in blue coveralls hauling our furniture away. I remember the whiff of alcohol on my father's breath, and soon violent arguments with my mom about lost paychecks and his elusive whereabouts in the evenings. Then he was gone—and now suddenly he had reappeared, a stranger passing through town on his way to a sales convention in San Diego. My father.

At the end of Scott Road, I stopped at an ornate wrought-iron gate and entered a code the doctor had given me. The gate swung open without a sound.

I drove through wide, twisting streets—Cabrini Drive, Via Venezia, Via Verona—with towering homes, fringed by lavender, rosemary, and cypress, like ships riding sculpted half acres. The doctor's home, on the leveled top of a steep hill, looked over the quivering grid of the San Fernando Valley. The home's tile roof and arched porticos reminded me of a Tuscan villa. I could see into the living room. A single lamp projected a moody light over the walls and furniture.

I parked across the street, obscured in the deep shadow of an untrimmed oleander that arched over the road, a place that offered a view of the front window and driveway. I scanned the radio for a station, mesmerized by the racing indigo numbers, as if they were a code. The dial stopped. A man with a deep baritone voice argued for a preemptive military strike against North Korea. I reclined the seat until my eyes were just above the bottom of the window, so anyone looking out from the house would see an empty car. The commentator's voice pitched higher as he squabbled with a caller who didn't share his opinion. I wondered if my father had gone to bed.

Earlier, when Eric called, I was grateful for an excuse to leave. I could have reached out to another one of

my investigators, paid him a little more for the inconvenience. Someone would have gone. But as I listened to
my father, oblivious and unrepentant, I feared I might
say something accusatory and cutting. Or worse—I
feared I might haul him out of his chair to ask if he'd ful-
filled the spiritual journey he described in the short note
we found on the kitchen countertop. I wanted to convey
to him in precise detail about our lives after he left: the
bleak cinder block apartment complex off the 170 in
North Hollywood, its echoing hallways and stairwells
that oozed the sour vapor of cigarettes and mildew; the
first job my mom landed, without a college degree or
professional skills, in the sweltering laundry of a linen
and uniform supplier in Van Nuys, how maggots from
bloody scrubs and soiled hospital sheets would crawl up
her arms as she loaded the washers; and later, how as a
receptionist at a plastics manufacturer in Pacoima she
felt insignificant and marginalized, relegated by her boss
to answer phones and sort mail during company parties
and events. And for me, the stigma of free lunches and
thrift store clothes and food stamps. And the insatiable
hunger I felt for years. Not for food or drink—but for
him. His presence. His voice. How could he cut us from
his life so quickly, seemingly without regret and pain? As
a husband and father, the thought confounded me.

Suddenly, another light turned on in the doctor's
living room, jolting me from my gloomy thoughts. She
was there, the doctor's wife, standing at the large picture
window in a purple bathrobe, her face illuminated by

the ground lights in the yard. Her brown hair hung over her shoulders, tangled from sleep, as she stared into the night with puffy eyes. She stooped under the weight of something in her arms. Lifting my hand slowly, as if a quick movement might disrupt the scene, I framed her in the viewfinder and pressed record.

▪■■▪

It was past two when I started for home.

Rain beaded the windshield. My breath fogged the glass. I felt as if I were overheating in the car's stale air. I cracked the window, and a cold wind steeped with the mineral odor of wet pavement hit me. Above, the dingy sky was the color of steel wool.

I stopped at Glenoaks and Magnolia, waiting for the red light to turn. The roads were empty. The light changed to green, to yellow, and then to red. I idled there with my foot on the brake, watching the sequence again and again. The colors bled across the drenched asphalt, a warped likeness of the world.

At home, I quietly opened the front door and walked carefully through the dark living room. Light filtered through the rain-streaked picture window, projecting watery shadows across the wood floors. Allison's potted palms and English ivy cast strange, distorted silhouettes over the walls. The smell of cooked meat lingered in the air. I heard a muffled sound. The blood pulsed in my ears.

"Troy."

My father slouched in the leather loveseat, a bottle in his hand. I felt anger slip in behind the fright. "Are you drinking?" I asked.

"This?" my father said, raising the bottle. He laughed. "No, this is supposed to be some new age miracle cure a friend got me on. Stronger immune system, mental clarity, deeper sleep. All for a price." He breathed out a tired, raspy sigh. "I just want to sleep through the night again. Your mother could fall asleep in a minute. A clear conscience, that's why." He pointed to the sectional. "Stay a couple minutes with your old man."

I forced myself to sit.

"So how'd it go?" he asked.

I stared at his hand gripping the bottle. "What?"

"The surveillance. The mother strung out on drugs."

"Long. Boring."

"So what happened?" he asked. "Smoking gun?"

"That's Hollywood," I said, "the stuff of movies."

"But still, you get the bad guys, right?" My father leaned forward. "I have friends whose kids are teachers, lawyers, dentists, boring stuff like that. But when I tell them you're a private investigator, they're interested. They want specifics."

I noticed how the shadows of the water coursing down the window twined together and cast an enormous net over my father. I rubbed my eyes, wondering what grand, inflated image of me he'd constructed for his friends.

"Like that murder case you did," he said. "The skin-heads who killed that Mexican kid in Riverside. I even recorded the interview you did for *Dateline*." He set the bottle on the slatted top of the oak coffee table, next to a stack of Allison's *Good Housekeeping* magazines. In the silvery light, the bottle and the magazines appeared like a sepia still-life painting.

"Why are you here?" I asked. "Do you need something? Money?"

For a moment, my father didn't say anything, and I wondered if he'd heard me.

"I wanted to see you and Allison," he finally said. "I wanted to meet my grandsons. And maybe I thought you and I could talk."

"About what?" I asked, hardly recognizing my voice. "What do you want? Forgiveness?"

"I don't know," my father said. "Maybe there's no forgiveness. I thought we could sit and talk like two men who know people make mistakes they regret forever. I don't want to pretend I didn't hurt you and your mom. What I did, leaving like that, I think about it every day."

A car passed slowly, water slushing under its tires. Headlights raked across the living room walls, briefly catching my father's tired, boney face. He blinked, then held his eyes shut, but not before I saw their heavy sadness. That sadness. I marveled at its sudden familiarity since I'd become a bishop, staring at me from the other side of my office desk at church, spread over weary, burdened faces waiting for me to utter a reassuring word.

I stood and walked to the window, peering through the streams of water on the glass. The wet pavement glowed under the streetlamps. I wanted to leave, to retreat up the stairs and into the oblivion of sleep. But something held me there. In some way, the glow of the streetlamps and the slushing tires of the passing car, like the hum of a crowd, brought suddenly to my mind warm summer nights, the smell of cut grass and the glow of stadium lights.

I was so close to the window my breath formed small circles on the glass. I knew anyone looking in couldn't see us.

"When we lived in La Crescenta," I said, "remember what happened when you found out the city didn't have a Little League? It became your cause. You went to city council meetings. You wrote letters to the chamber of commerce. You got businesses to donate money for uniforms and equipment. You found a coach."

My father laughed. "I charmed them. Or maybe I was just a pain in the old backside. But how could I let all your raw talent go to waste? Lightening on the bases. A lethal arm in the outfield. Don't get me started about you."

I touched the window. It felt glacial against my open palm. "Near the end of my mission, I was in this little ward outside Baton Rouge. I don't know why, but my companion and I had to speak on Father's Day. Who asks missionaries to speak on Father's Day? It made no sense. And what could I say, me without a father? Do you know what I talked about? How you started Little League in La Crescenta. After what you did to us, that's what I talked about. My companion was this rich kid from Minneapolis, dad a big executive at Target. With all he said about his dad in that talk, how great he was, he told me that night how his dad would never have spent all that time and gone through all the trouble. He was almost crying when he said it. He envied me. Can you believe that? He was jealous of us—of you."

Behind me, I heard the rustle of fabric and the crack of knees, and then my father's steps moving toward me. He stood at my side, breathing heavily.

"The woman, the doctor's wife," I said, "she didn't know I was there. I'm sure of it." The rain was coming harder, peeling the dead leaves from the asphalt and pushing them into the gutters. My reflection smeared and shuddered with the movement of the water on the glass. "You know what she was doing? Rocking her three-year-old son to sleep. Singing songs. Wiping his nose. That's what I got. Three hours of it."

"Then it's over," my father said. "Case closed."

"It's not like that," I said. "He'll pay us to keep watching until she does something his lawyer can misconstrue or exaggerate. That's what I do."

My father shook his head. "It seems like a strange business. I guess I really don't understand your work, Troy."

"You don't understand?" I laughed. "I'm a voyeur. I look for what people want to forget. I hope people do terrible things so my clients are happy."

"But they're guilty, right?" my father asked. "I mean, there has to be a reason."

I felt exhausted. "Sure, most are. But the truth is"—I hesitated—"the truth is, if I had to, I could find something on anyone. Everyone has something."

"Seems like a line of work that lends itself to pessimism," my father said. He paused, then tipped his head back and laughed. "I just thought, what if some guy came to your office tomorrow and hired you to find the good in someone? Wouldn't that turn the business upside down?"

"No money in it," I said.

"I'm just speaking in the hypothetical," my father said. "Say this guy walks into your office, gives you a name and address, and hires you to find some good in this person. Video, photographic evidence, whatever. You know, make a case for it. Could you do it?"

"I guess, if I wanted to," I said.

"And let's say," my father said, tapping a knuckle against the cold glass, "that this is the address, your address, and the guy wants you to sit outside the house, on a night just like this, to watch a father and son talking like we are. Do you think you could find some good, maybe just a little, in the father?"

"It'd be too hard," I said. "Without lights, I couldn't see a thing."

"But what if you could?" my father said, an insistence in his voice I'd never heard before. "What if you could see it all perfectly, the son standing where you are, and the father standing next to the son, not knowing someone's watching?"

Rubbing my eyes, as if that might help me see better, I said: "Dad, after so long, I don't know if I care anymore." And then I stepped away from the window.

I watched my father, who stood like a statue, unaware I was no longer at his side. He reached his arm into the space where I'd stood, smiling sheepishly at his reflection as his arm fell into emptiness. I sat down heavily on the loveseat and pulled at my collar. I felt restricted, caught in the shifting net of watery shadows working down the walls and across my body, knowing that the camera beyond the dark window, meant to find a little good, wouldn't be fixed on my father. But on me.

Adam and Lilith. And Eve

God took Adam and the woman on a walking tour of the garden he'd planted for them eastward in Eden. "You're going to love this!" God said. "Grass and herb-yielding seeds and fruit trees of every kind. Eat from any of the trees, just not that one with the round, red fruit." Then God raised his mighty arms in the air and spun around, the hem of his white robe rising in a perfect circle. "And look at the hills and the forests and the meadows, all for you. What do you think?"

"Wonderful," Adam said. "Just fabulous. I'm speechless. All this abundant goodness. We love it, right?" He nodded to the woman.

She gazed out over a grassy clearing rimmed with broad, towering trees. "It's nice," she said, "but all the green's, like, a little overwhelming. Don't you think?

How about a touch of red and yellow? Maybe some wild flowers?"

Adam felt a sudden burst of tepid moisture pooling in his armpits.

"And what about opening things up to let in more light?" the woman continued. "Feels so cramped. Then some boulders for sitting and maybe a pond with a waterfall. Running water really calms the mind."

God tipped his bearded chin up and puffed out his broad chest. "Didn't you see the four rivers to water the garden?" He nudged Adam with his elbow. "How's that for water? And get a load of these names." God smiled as he fluttered his raised hands. "The Pison, Havilah, Gihon, and Hiddekel."

The woman bit her lip and snorted.

God's hands flopped to his sides. "Something wrong?" he asked.

The woman shook her head. "Those are the weirdest names."

Adam scratched his neck and laughed nervously. "I don't think she means weird. Weird's such a strong word. Maybe uncommon? Or how about unique?"

"No," the woman said. "I mean weird. Who'd want to take a moonlit stroll on the Hiddekel River? Who'd want to picnic on the mighty Gihon? What about the Serenity River or the River Felicity?"

God's brow furrowed. He looked hurt. "I thought the names sounded strong, authoritative, grand—"

"You mean masculine?" the woman interrupted.

God sighed. "Well, it's your world, Adam. Name the rivers what you want. In fact, give everything a name." He pointed to the woman. "Even her."

"His world?" the woman protested, two fisted hands suddenly planted on her naked hips. "And I'll choose my own name, thank you very much."

Adam crossed his arms. "Eve," he said, wanting God to see he could handle this woman. "I'll call you Eve."

The woman let out a retching sound. "Eve! Ugh!" Her right hand shot up from her hip. She pointed at Adam. "You'll call me Lilith."

God cleared his throat. "Wow, look at the time," he said, tapping the gold watch on his thick wrist. "I'd love to stay and chat, but I have to talk to my oldest son about his role as Savior of Mankind." God clasped his hands together. "So, Adam, I'm putting you in charge of this garden, the fish, the birds, everything. And"— God winked—"I want you to multiply and replenish the earth."

"We won't disappoint you," Adam shouted through cupped hands as God ascended into heaven.

Lilith closed her eyes and made wet kissing noises, then doubled over with laughter.

Adam frowned. "What?"

·◼·◼·

Adam spent the rest of that first day surveying the garden, fording streams and trekking over steep, wooded hills, naming the creatures and plants he found. He'd decided to devote eighteen hours a day to his garden duties. Maybe he'd even finish naming everything by the end of the week. He could just imagine God's pleased astonishment, how he'd say something like, "It took me six days to create the earth and you named everything in less than a week!" Then he'd tousle Adam's sandy hair and declare, "My boy, this just proves you're my greatest creation."

Later that afternoon Adam found Lilith next to a shaded brook that bubbled over smooth stones. She was bent in a strange position: hips fixed to the ground, legs extended, her back arched unnaturally. Then she shot up onto her toes and hands, her body forming a perfect V. A low humming sound vibrated in her throat.

"What are you doing?" Adam asked. He couldn't help notice the curved, sculpted lines of Lilith's calves and the hard swell of her triceps, and how his own arms seemed puny compared to hers.

Lilith stood, raising both hands high above her head while breathing deeply through her mouth. "I call it yoga. I pretend I'm an animal or a tree or a mountain. It's a totally awesome way to relieve stress patterns and relax the mind. You should try it!"

Adam wiped at his damp forehead with the back of his hand. "Too much to do. You have any idea how big this garden is?"

"It's amazing, isn't it?" Lilith said. "Have you noticed how the wind moving through the trees sounds like rushing water? Or those little tube creatures in the ground—"

"Worms," Adam interrupted. "I'm calling them worms."

"Worms, then," Lilith said. "How worms make, like, this faint popping noise when they wiggle out of their holes. And look at that huge mountain over there. What's that white stuff on top?" Her eyes widened. She licked her lips. "Should we find out?"

Adam shook his head. "I've barely named half the creatures and plants. So much work to do, so little time. I'm sure you can imagine the weight of my responsibilities." He regarded his reflection in the brook, the beautiful symmetry of his face and the bow of delicate blond hair sweeping across his forehead. "But I guess that's just the sacrifice you make when the all-powerful creator of the universe gives you dominion over all things and commands you to subdue the earth."

"Yeah, I get it," Lilith said. "You're very important."

Adam nodded. He wouldn't argue with that—but there was something he'd been meaning to bring up with Lilith.

"So, I'm sure you remember God's command to multiply and replenish the earth?" Adam said. "Well, the last thing I'd want is to disappoint God. I'm sure you feel the same way." He pointed to the tuft of wiry hair between Lilith's legs. "Now, I'm not exactly sure how this works, but I think I'm supposed to insert my—"

Lilith took a step back. "Buy a girl a drink first, will you!"

"What's wrong?" Adam said.

"I mean, sure, you're an attractive guy"—Lilith looked Adam up and down—"though your core and upper arms could use some work. And I'd really tone down the egomania crap."

Adam felt his brow crease and the sides of his mouth droop. "Well, God's perfect and he created me in his image. I don't think it gets any better."

"Sure, an impressive pedigree," Lilith said, "but I'm, like, not really into that whole pedigree thing. Plus, there's too much to do and see. Who wants to be tied down?" She placed two fingers to her neck. "Well, I need to get my heart rate up. See you around."

Adam watched Lilith jog up a short hill and disappear over its grassy crest.

"Swing and a miss!" a man said, ambling out from behind a sprawling bush. He wore a black leather jacket over a white T-shirt, thick steel-toed boots crisscrossed by three silver buckles, and dark jeans rolled up to his boot tops. His slicked-back hair had an oily sheen.

"Who are you?" Adam asked.

The man extended his hand. "Well, I have lots of names, but my friends call me Snake." His palm felt smooth and eerily cool, and he exuded the faint odor of garlic.

"Do you live here?" Adam asked. "I thought it was just me and the woman. Lilith. Whatever her name is."

Snake raised his hands as if surrendering. "Hey, I'm just as surprised as you. This place ain't my style, man. I like heat and endless, barren stretches of sand and rock and dirt. Thing is, the old man didn't dig me, kicked me out. What a square. Said I was a bad influence. So I might crash here for a while, if that's cool." He winked at Adam, then flicked his chin in the direction Lilith had gone. "Your girl cut out on you, man, told you she didn't want none of your mojo?" Snake raised the collar of his jacket.

"You mean Lilith?" Adam said. "I don't think she wants anything to do with me. I don't even think she likes me."

"The thoroughbreds are like that," Snake said, squinting until his eyes were just two dark slits slashed across his face. "Unless you know how to handle all that horsepower." Snake cracked his knuckles. "Hey, you wouldn't mind if I, like, asked her out, man?"

"Good luck with that," Adam said.

Snake pulled a plastic comb from his back pocket and slid it through his oily mane. "Right on, Daddy-O."

▪■▪■▪

That night Adam ventured out to name some of the nocturnal animals. Fruit bat, gray wolf, bush rat, white-tailed deer—all sensible, practical names he thought God would like. Earlier, he'd let Lilith take a shot at this naming thing, thinking with her help he'd finish up by the end of the week—though he'd immediately regretted his decision. Aardvark, kangaroo, wombat, possum. Who'd ever heard of such ridiculous names?

At about midnight, in a grove of trees overlooked by a slick, stony embankment, Adam found Snake sitting on a boulder, hunched over and staring at the ground.

"Hey, man," Snake said, his voice flat, each word punctuated by a moist sniffle. His hair was matted and disheveled, littered with grass and dirt. The neck of his white T-shirt sagged. Adam wondered if he'd somehow toppled over the embankment, until he saw an angry red welt the exact shape of a hand on Snake's cheek.

"Lilith?" Adam asked, wincing as Snake lifted his head to reveal a swollen eye the exact color of a ripe plum.

Two lines of snot glistened above his quivering lips. "She's such a meanie. A big dumb meanie," Snake said, his voice a whimper.

A spattering of small, fuzzy stars danced across Adam's vision. He turned away from Snake's battered face and took a sudden interest in the bright moon winking through the upper branches of the trees.

"Why'd she have to treat me like that?" Snake asked, gazing up at Adam with one dark, pleading eye. Snake grabbed a passing squirrel that had stopped to investigate the noise and wiped his nose with it, then tossed the animal over his shoulder. "I thought she was really into me. I was like, 'Baby, that's some tan, or do you always look this hot?' And she was like, 'Hot?' And I was like, 'Yeah, baby, scorching my eyeballs hot. And that's a nice ass. It's a shame you have to sit on it.' And she's looking at me and like, 'Some tan? A nice ass?' And I'm thinking it's a good sign that she's kinda repeating back everything, like she's digging it. So I go on, and I'm like, 'Baby, I wrote a poem for you. It goes like this: My name is Snake. It might sound corny, but you make me horny. I'll give you a hiss if you give me a kiss.' And since I thought she was into the jam, I tried to kiss her." Snake brought both hands to his cheeks, as if he were trying to steady his head. "And then boom, like a tree fell on me, man, bright lights, and then I'm on the ground, and she's over me waving her fist, and yelling something like, 'I refuse to be an embellishment or an ornament. I am not an object of your sexual desire.'" Snake wept loudly into his palms. "What does that even mean, man? I just wanted to tell her she's hot."

▪■▪■▪

The next morning Adam awoke coughing violently. A pall of thick smoke slid through the trees, catching in his throat and stinging his eyes. Panicked, he trailed the smoke to a clearing where Lilith sat next to a small fire, holding a stick over the leaping flames. There was something on the stick, a brown mass that sizzled and popped.

Adam's heart knocked in his chest. He could barely catch his breath. "I thought the garden was on fire!"

"Don't get your panties in a bunch," Lilith said, her eyes fixed on the stick. "It's almost done."

Adam squinted at the stick. "What is that? Fruit?" But he suddenly knew, a realization that squeezed at his guts and filled his mouth with a sour taste. Whatever was on the stick looked oddly familiar: the oblong skull and stubby tail. And what was that white, red-flecked thing at Lilith's feet?

Lilith turned the stick slowly in the fire. Juices dripped onto the glowing embers and hissed. "This? It's one of those fluffy things. What did you call it? A rabbit?"

Adam covered his face with both hands, peering to the heavens through the thin spaces between his fingers, suddenly terrified that God might be watching them. He spoke in a whisper. "You killed a rabbit? God didn't say anything about killing the animals. We're supposed to name them, not eat them."

"Hey, I don't know about you," Lilith said, "but I've had the screaming craps ever since we got here. It's all this fruit. Fruit, fruit, fruit. Breakfast, lunch, and dinner. I need protein to build muscle mass." She took a huge bite of the rabbit, her eyes closing in ecstasy. A trickle of grease oozed down her chin, through her ample breasts, and pooled in her bellybutton. "Oh, this is good." She waved Adam over. "Try some."

Adam had to admit the cooked rabbit smelled delicious, and the sight of Lilith smacking her greasy lips made his stomach growl and gurgle. He was beginning to feel the same way about their all-fruit diet. His bowel movements had been less than firm, coming explosively every hour or two. Still, God hadn't said anything about eating the animals, the very animals they had dominion over.

Lilith dangled the rabbit in front of Adam. "Sounds like somebody's hungry. Take a bite. Come on."

"Lilith," Adam said firmly. "God didn't say anything about eating the animals. We're supposed to watch over them, protect them."

"Now about that," Lilith said, gnawing at the rabbit's shoulder. "God's great, and he gave us this really cool garden, but it just doesn't seem fair that some distant patriarchal figure should enforce, like, some autocratic moral system that we don't have a say in. I mean, we're down here, and God's up there, doing whatever it is he does, so shouldn't we, like, make our own rules?"

"Well," Adam said, standing a little taller, "since God put me in charge, I can certainly pass along your concerns and suggestions."

"You're, like, so cute when you get all hierarchical," Lilith said. "But seriously, maybe we should really think about, like, deconstructing patriarchy and then, like, constructing some social system that's more equitable and based on our own empirical knowledge and experiences. You know, like a more pragmatic approach."

Adam turned away from Lilith, suddenly feeling the strong pulse of a vein in his forehead and a rising heat spreading through his neck and face. His molars ground together.

·■·■·

The next afternoon, God and Adam were walking together in the garden.

"Well, I did just what you asked," Adam said. He'd barely slept in the last five days, working through the nights. His arms and legs felt heavy and unwieldy, throbbing with a dull ache. "I named every beast of the field and fowl of the air and fish of the sea, and every creeping thing that creepeth upon the earth. All the plants and trees. Everything."

But God just stared at a distant bloom of dense, silvery clouds and tugged pensively at his long beard.

"Do you think I'm portly?" God asked.

Adam was confused. He wondered if this was some kind of test. "Portly? Not a chance. I'd say sturdy, firm, hearty. But not portly."

God nodded, considering Adam's words. "Do you think I have a stiff walk?"

"No way," Adam said. "I'd say your walk is kingly, majestic, noble." Adam gave God a quick side-glance, then looked at the ground. "Is something wrong?"

God clucked his tongue. "It's just Lilith. We were talking yesterday, and she said, 'God, can I tell you something?' And I said sure, expecting her to thank me for all the beautiful, pleasant things I created. But instead, she's like, 'I'm just a little worried about you. Do you snack between meals? Are you getting enough exercise? Because that might explain why you're a little portly.' And then she said, 'And I've noticed you kind of have a stiff walk. It might be tight hamstrings, maybe from sitting too much on your heavenly throne.' And then for the next hour she was bending me this way and that, and she kept saying strange things like double pigeon and open lizard and downward dog. It's just that I'm kind of a big deal in the universe and not accustomed to people bending me into weird shapes and telling me to breathe deeply."

Adam swallowed hard. "God, I don't want you to think I'm ungrateful, because I'm not. You made an awesome world with lots of really cool stuff, and I'm so honored to be part of it. It's just that I don't think Lilith's working out. She's not really into rules and respecting my authority or yours, and she's always going on about sunsets and what the air smells like after it rains and the sound of wind in the trees. And worst, she doesn't want to multiply and replenish the earth with me. Maybe something went wrong with her, not that you'd ever mess up, God. No way. But maybe something fell in the mix when your back was turned, or maybe one of the ingredients was a little old."

God breathed out a long sigh. "Sometimes I worry too much about what people think of me, so maybe I shouldn't even tell you this. It's just that when I finished creating you, you fell asleep in my arms, and you looked so peaceful, your ruddy cheeks and pouty lips. I knew I should take one of your ribs to create a woman, but I didn't want to wake you up, and I thought taking a rib would really be painful and, frankly, a little yucky. Blood totally grosses me out. Instead, I took some dust from a passing comet to create Lilith. Maybe I really messed up."

Adam touched God's elbow. "Hey, that's all right. I still think you're great."

God brushed away a tear that had fallen in his beard. "That means a lot to me. Really. It's like everyone always thinks, 'Hey, it's God. He doesn't need a compliment now and then. He created the universe.' But I do."

The watch on God's wrist chimed. "Wow, it's that time already. I need to meet with my oldest son again about this Savior of Mankind business. With all the sweating great drops of blood and flogging and crucifixion, it's been a hard sell. Well, let's talk later about this Lilith business."

And with that, God was off.

▪■■▪

A couple days later Adam was inventorying the animals. He checked and rechecked his ledger, but for some reason mammal numbers were down.

"Hey!"

Adam turned quickly, astonished that an animal he'd never seen before was walking upright toward him. It was covered from head to toe with thick fur. And then Adam peered at the face, suddenly recognizing Lilith. He stared and pointed, a wh-wh-wh sound wheezing through his lips, until he could form some coherent words. "What are you wearing?"

"You like?" Lilith said, turning slowly. "It's fur, like from animals. Feel how soft it is. And so warm."

Adam's body stiffened. He scanned the tapestry of fur, his lips mouthing names: beaver, fox, wolf, mink, and those adorable raccoons. An entire skinned coyote sat atop Lilith's head, one flaccid paw dangling over her right shoulder.

An emptiness shot up from Adam's stomach and washed over him. He'd failed. God had commanded him to subdue the earth, had given him dominion over all things, and he couldn't even subdue this woman, who was ruining everything, challenging his authority, breaking the social order, and eating and wearing the animals. Adam swallowed hard and blinked quickly to stay the hot moisture pooling in his eyes.

Lilith flicked the dangling coyote paw over her shoulder. "Well, I'm off to see the world," she said. Her eyes had a distant look. She tipped her head up, like an animal on a scent, and took a deep breath. "Don't you ever just turn to the wind and take in all the smells, and you know they're from some faraway place you've never been? That's where I'm going, to all those places."

"You're leaving?" Adam felt a sudden lightness in his chest. A haze cleared from the edges of his vision. Leaving? The woman was leaving. Adam interlaced his fingers, feeling a sudden need to pump his fists in the air. "Well, it's been a pleasure," he said solemnly, bowing slightly. "Best of luck out there."

"I was kind of hoping you'd come along," Lilith said. "We'll see it together."

Adam gazed at the distant mountains, dark and skirted by foreboding clouds, so high, so imposing. His hands trembled. "I don't think so. God didn't say anything about leaving the garden."

"Oh, that's right," Lilith said, smiling. Her eyes sparkled. "I almost forgot: you're God's most obedient creation."

▪■▪■▪

Soon after Lilith left, God created another woman, this time from one of Adam's ribs. The procedure wasn't painful, just some soreness for a couple days and a small, glossy scar that Adam thought made him look tough.

He called the woman Eve, a name she accepted without protest. She was blonde and petite, soft and curvy in all the right places, super deferential to his authority, and totally on board with multiplying and replenishing the earth.

If only the easy living in the garden, though, could have gone on forever: branches forever bowing with ripe fruit, docile animals frolicking at their feet, and walks with God on Sunday afternoons. It wasn't long before Snake came slinking around again, feeding Eve some line about how sexy the forbidden fruit was, just like her, and how just one tiny bite would make her like God.

Well, that really pissed off God—like anyone could ever be as powerful and glorious as him—so he banished Eve to the dark and dreary world. Adam felt awful, watching Eve shiver and cry and go on and on about how all that sweating and planting and weeding in the fallen world would ruin her hair and nails. So Adam ate the fruit, too, just so Eve wouldn't be alone.

Soon enough, Adam learned that the fallen world is a real bitch.

All the thorns and thistles—Adam could barely keep up. And the animals he'd once named and tickle-wrestled in the lush, verdant meadows of Eden were always stealing his corn—or trying to eat him.

God never came around anymore, never wanted to take a Sunday walk, just shouted down from heaven or from some cloud-coiled mountain. Do this and do that. Worship only me. Don't labor on the Sabbath. Sacrifice the firstlings of your flock—as if good sheep grew on trees. "And if you don't do everything I ask," God would shout, "then I'll curse you with plagues of lice and frogs, and your cattle's teeth will fall out, and I'll afflict you with hemorrhoids." It seemed God was always angry about something.

And too often Snake would just show up unannounced around dinnertime. He'd traded in the leather jacket and black boots for a double-breasted suit and a pair of Armani calfskin loafers, and he'd sit by the fire, watching Eve over his Ray-Bans, and go on about his latest business venture, selling spray-on vitamins or timeshare condos in Phoenix, and how his downline was earning him six figures a year, and how he could set Adam up, if he wanted, really put some dough in his pocket to feed and clothe all those little bodies. Adam didn't like the way Snake ogled Eve's breasts and shapely backside—though he couldn't help thinking that maybe Eve liked the attention, the way she batted her eyes and canted her hips a little more whenever Snake showed up. And why wouldn't she? Why wouldn't she prefer some cocky bad boy with a two thousand dollar suit to him, a working man who smelled like cow dung and sour arm-pits?

So six days a week, sunup to sundown, earning his bread by the sweat of his brow, Adam worked. The kids—dozens of them, so many he couldn't keep them straight—were so needy and mischievous, especially that Cain, the way he was always shoving acorns up Abel's nose or inflicting super wedgies, and then blaming his sisters. Adam wished Eve would take a firmer hand disci-plining the kids, but she was just so timid—and gullible.

Sometimes Adam would point to the sky and say, "Sky looks green today, doesn't it?" Eve would say, "Sure does." And then Adam would say, "Actually, it looks kind of red." Eve would squint up at the sky again and say, "Yes, red. Now I see it." Then Adam would say, "Well, what color do you think the sky is?" And without fail, Eve would cozy up to him with that sexy smile, comb her fin-gers through his golden chest hair, and trill warmly in his ear, "I'm really more interested in your opinions." Well, if Eve was gullible to a fault, at least it comforted Adam that she made a really tasty gruel and always gave his loincloths an extra rock beating so they wouldn't chafe his balls on hot days.

Still, some nights as Adam sat next to the fire, the flickering light pushing at the darkness, he couldn't help but think of Lilith and smile. Eve would look up from her nail file and ask why he was grinning. Adam would belch quietly into his hand and tell her it was nothing, just a little gas from the mastodon brisket and tuber mash she'd made for dinner.

Lilith, with all her strong opinions and whimsical observations, challenging God and throttling Snake. Sometimes while gazing at the sharp peak of a distant mountain, Adam wondered where Lilith had gone, and every so often, when the moon hung like a luminous disk in the sky, he thought he heard her somewhere out there in the great big world, a howl of pure, contagious ecstasy, as free and wild as wind moving through the treetops.

The Lord's Sacred Funds

Bishop Bruce Horkley of the Burbank 4th Ward sat at his desk rehearsing for the sacrament meeting he'd preside over in thirty minutes. He wanted his delivery of the weekly announcements to be flawless and spiritually evocative. *And Thursday night, the Relief Society will have a quilting project.* The timbre of his voice must be solemn and apostolic. *The annual Boy Scout Pancake Breakfast fundraiser will be this Saturday at nine.* He slowed his tempo to emphasize each syllable, as if every halting word, no matter how mundane, bore a weight on his soul that might bring him to tears at any moment. *And the Red Cross blood drive will be next Thursday at the Riverside building. All donors will receive a coupon for a free pint of Baskin Robbins ice cream.*

Bishop Horkley raised his chin and fixed his narrowed eyes on the ceiling, mouth slightly agape, an expression, somewhere between euphoria and indigestion, he'd worked on all month in his bathroom mirror.

Suddenly, there were three soft knocks at the office door.

Bishop Horkley smiled, silently congratulating himself for the foresight to lock the door. A month ago, his first administrative decision as the new bishop was to stop paying Sister Peterson's premium cable package. Dale Carney, his second counselor, had pled the old woman's case: "She's eighty-eight years old, Bishop, lives on a fixed income, and doesn't have family for five hundred miles. She gets a little lonely. She keeps the TV on all day just to feel like somebody's home with her." Bishop Horkley rattled the cable bill in his hand. "But the premium cable package?" he asked. "HBO. Cinemax. Showtime. What's wrong with basic cable? What's wrong with *The Merv Griffin Show* and *Bonanza* reruns? Have you seen the quality programming on PBS? *Antique Roadshow. This Old House. New Scandinavian Cooking.*" Bishop Horkley brought a closed fist down on his desk. "Brother Carney, these are the Lord's sacred funds!"

Sister Peterson had called the next day, begging the bishop to at least let her finish the last season of *Game of Thrones* before he cut her off. Bishop Horkley was unmoved. And now he suspected the old lady was dropping by his church office to argue her case in person.

There were three more knocks at the door. And then, as if acted upon by an unseen hand, the lock mechanism clicked and the door handle turned. A bearded man, with thick brown hair parted down the middle, stood in the doorway. He wore sandals and what looked like a white linen bathrobe.

Bishop Horkley rose from behind the desk, his hand involuntarily brushing over his bald, speckled head, a habit he had when seeing a man with luxuriant hair.

"Excuse me." The bishop gave his words a flinty edge, hoping this man—obviously homeless and certainly insane and no doubt sniffing around for a few bucks—would catch the irritation in his voice.

Bishop Horkley suspected the word was on the streets about the new Mormon bishop in Burbank, whispered through some skid-row grapevine or penned on dingy bathroom stalls. For the last month, they'd come in droves each Sunday—the insane, the homeless, the indigent—hoping for a pushover and an easy handout. There'd been a legless man in a Jazzy wheelchair painted with red racing stripes, a deranged old woman with a kitten in her purse that she'd occasionally pull out and lick, and a whole family of gypsies—real gypsies with gold teeth and accordions—who needed some money, not much, they said, just enough to buy a high-definition TV and a Hulu subscription. "I'm sorry," Bishop Horkley had told all of them with a stern finality, "but these are the Lord's sacred funds."

The bearded man didn't say anything; with a half smile, he just stared at Bishop Horkley with brown, amiable—or crazy—eyes that absorbed him and everything in the office at a glance. The gaze unsettled Bishop Horkley, who began to wonder if this man had picked the lock and entered his office to steal something—or even to do him bodily harm.

"Are you looking for someone?" the bishop asked. His heart thudded against his crisply pressed white shirt.

"I'm looking for you," the man said. "You don't recognize me?"

Bishop Horkley's glutes clenched, in case he had to vault the desk and shoulder his way through the office door. He'd heard about this before, some jilted homeless case, denied a handout, returning for vengeance. He stared at the man—who did look vaguely familiar—trying to place him. Had he stopped by in the last month for a handout? Bishop Horkley couldn't remember.

"*Do* I know you?" the bishop asked.

"Well, I hope so," the man said. He stepped into the office, and, with a quick swipe of a finger through the air, the heavy door closed. Then the man turned his hands to show his palms. "I'm Jesus Christ."

Bishop Horkley gaped at the nail prints. "Lord, I'm so sorry. I didn't recognize—" And then a thought struck the bishop. He pivoted to look out his office window. "Is this the Second Coming?" he asked. "The end of times? The final judgment?" The bishop took in the great sprawl of the San Fernando Valley overlaid with a golden haze of pollution and particulate matter. In the distance, car windshields winked brightly on the I-5. Jetliners roared out of Bob Hope Airport. Forest Lawn Cemetery appeared placid and pastoral, ropes of silvery water arcing from the sprinklers. No open graves and risen dead. No engulfing fire over the Hollywood Hills. No dark horsemen charging up Sunset Canyon Drive.

Jesus laughed. "It's not quite the end yet—though I get that all the time. No, I just like to get out sometimes to visit my flock."

Bishop Horkley was relieved it wasn't the end of the world—he was only one month into his five-year tenure as bishop. "I see," he said, not knowing the etiquette for divine visitation. Should he offer up his cushioned, high-backed leather chair and take one of the wooden chairs lining the office wall? The sight of the wooden chairs, the uninviting dark stripes of lacquered oak grain and the sharp, perfect angles of the armrests, sent a flash of hot sciatic pain down Bishop Horkley's right thigh.

The bishop causally rested a hand on the high leather back of his chair, a subtle, proprietary gesture. And why would Jesus need a soft chair? he thought. As a resurrected being, couldn't he sit comfortably on a bed of nails?

"So," Bishop Horkley said, trying to fill the silence.

"May I sit?" the Lord finally asked, motioning to one of the wooden chairs.

Bishop Horkley was relieved. "Of course. Please."

Jesus sat and crossed his right leg over his left. "I want to attend your meetings today. I want to instruct and bless the members of the Burbank 4th Ward." Jesus raised his arms. "If their faith is sufficient, maybe I'll even do some healing."

Bishop Horkley was distracted. He couldn't help staring at Jesus's long beard and sandals. It'd never occurred to him that the Savior of all men bore a striking resemblance to his third grade teacher, Mr. Blum, a bearded, Birkenstock-wearing, banjo-strumming hippie, a UC Berkeley grad who'd made the entire class march around the playground singing weepy dirges by Peter, Paul, and Mary. Even as an eight-year-old, the bishop didn't like the man's liberal, counterculture leanings.

"Oh, you want to stay for church?" Bishop Horkley asked. "For the entire time?"

"Yes. I think the ward members would enjoy it," Jesus said.

Bishop Horkley nodded. "Lord, let me just say that your presence among us—not just in spirit—would be a great blessing, never to be forgotten, I'm sure." He sucked in a mouthful of air and let it go with a low grunt. "It's just that—"

"You're worried about your congregation," Jesus said. "You feel my divine presence might overwhelm them at first?"

"Oh, no, no, nothing like that," Bishop Horkley said. "I've come down with an iron fist over the last month, really pounded into the members the need for reverence, punctuality, and modesty, daily scripture study, and prayer—otherwise they'll face damnation. No, Lord, I think they're worthy of your presence. It's just that . . . I wonder if what you're wearing, though I'm sure it was quite fashionable in ancient Palestine, might be slightly disruptive. I'm just concerned about some of our younger, more impressionable deacons. It's taken me a whole month just to get them to wear a full suit and vest. They see *you* and next Sunday I might have a dozen deacons show up for church in bathrobes and flip-flops. And the beard. I mean, it's not like in your day you could just run down to the Rite Aid in Nazareth to pick up a Gillette Fusion. But I fear the priests will see the beard as a license to become Grizzly Adams. No offense, Lord. These kids just don't understand historical context. That's my humble concern."

Jesus tugged at his beard. "Disruptive? You think so?"

"I do, Lord," Bishop Horkley said. "If we could move you just a baby step into the twenty-first century." The bishop reached into a desk drawer and pulled out a handful of ties, each sealed in a sleeve of clear, sterile plastic. "I bought them from a discount bin at Walmart. Ten ties for ten bucks. What a deal! Say what you want about the Chinese, but they make a darn good tie." The bishop slid one across the desk. "I think red's a good color for you."

Jesus eyed the tie suspiciously. "Well, okay. Thanks." He cleared his throat. "So I had this thought. For the sacrament, I want to perform a miracle: make a loaf of bread appear out of thin air. As the Bread of Life, I think members will appreciate the symbolism of the gesture. Then I'll break and bless the bread."

"Wow," Bishop Horkley said. "That *would* be memorable!" Then he looked at his hands. "It's just that—"

Jesus raised his eyebrows.

"I hesitate bringing it up," the bishop said, brushing away a speck of dust from the desktop. "It's just that I was wondering, Lord, if this miraculous loaf of bread could be, say, whole grain, gluten-free, and organic? Maybe a brown rice or quinoa? I feel silly even asking, but Sister Kipner will give me heck if even a molecule of gluten passes between her twins' lips."

"What are you saying?" Jesus asked.

Bishop Horkley clasped his hands together. "If it's not too much to ask, Lord, could we just stick with the Whole Foods organic tapioca bread we've been using?"

"No bread miracle?" Jesus's voice ticked up an octave.

"It would just mean fewer problems—for me," Bishop Horkley said. "Fewer complaints, fewer distractions as I humbly labor to lead this flock back to your presence. I just don't have the stomach for another of Sister Kipner's lectures on gut inflammation, intestinal permeability, and smelly stools."

"Well . . . okay," Jesus said, staring blankly at the desktop. "Then I'll just have to convey my infinite and everlasting love when I address the congregation. These are trying times. Many are struggling, physically, spiritually, emotionally, and financially. I hear it in their prayers. They're worried about crime, unemployment, global warming, overpopulation, gun control, health-care costs, illegal immigration, bio-warfare, terrorism, drought, earthquakes, clowns, infidelity, robots . . ."

Bishop Horkley nodded earnestly but was suddenly distracted by a thin, barely audible sound from the base-board behind his desk, a sound like a pair of tiny teeth gnawing on wood. Bishop Horkley's fingers coiled into tight fists. A rat in the Lord's house! Unthinkable!

"Prescription drug abuse," Jesus continued, "failing schools, social security, cyber bullying, erectile dysfunc-tion—"

"Is it a long message?" Bishop Horkley asked loudly, hoping to scare the rat away.

"What?" Jesus said.

"I mean"—the bishop drummed his knuckles against the desktop—"how many minutes? Two? Five? Ten? It's just that you picked one doozy of a Sunday to visit, Lord, though I'm so glad you're here, so honored by your presence. You see, I asked Brother and Sister Spears to speak, and if they don't get every second I promised them, I'll hear about it for the next three months. I'm sure you know what a pain in the keister they are." Bish-op Horkley snapped his fingers. "Hey, I wonder, Lord, if just your holy presence would be enough to convey that message of love and hope. I can see it now: you sitting on the stand, projecting goodness and love, but never say-ing a word, just a tear or two sliding down your cheeks.

I could even kind of lean over and put my arm over your shoulder. That would really drive it home."

"Just sit there and say nothing?" Jesus asked.

"*Silence is true wisdom's best reply,*" Bishop Horkley said. "I think that was Ronald Reagan. Powerful words from the Gipper."

Jesus uncrossed his legs. "Well, how about after sacrament meeting? I thought I'd visit the Primary children. You know, kind of like what I did in my earthly ministry."

Bishop Horkley pulled a white handkerchief from his breast pocket. "That story gets me every time." He dabbed at his moist eyes. "*Suffer the little children to come unto me, and forbid them not: for such is the kingdom of heaven.*"

"Yes, exactly," Jesus said, scooting to the edge of his chair, his voice animated. "I want to take the children up in my arms, put my hands on them and bless them—"

Bishop Horkley raised his palm. "No touching."

"What?" Jesus's broad shoulders drooped.

"No hugging. No lap sitting. It's just better not to touch them," Bishop Horkley said. "Parents freak out about that kind of stuff. And remember to prop open the classroom door so we can monitor what's going on. Church policy." Bishop Horkley patted the church's *General Handbook*, which sat on the corner of the desk. Its merlot cover and smooth finish comforted him. He found the same comfort in the dense insurance manuals he pored over at work, all the procedures and policies and rules safeguarding against chaos.

Bishop Horkley set his elbows on the desk and leaned forward. "And I'm assuming you've had a whooping cough vaccination?"

"Well, no," Jesus said, his head snapping up, his eyes wide and perplexed, "but I am a resurrected being. Isn't that enough?"

"I know, right?" Bishop Horkley shook his head. "But tell that to Sister Franklin, our Primary president, and to her six children, who've never tasted sugar, and to her hipster husband with that awful beard—no offense, Lord. The family's one big nut case. I swear they feel God's put them on this green earth with some liberal agenda to educate us about air-borne diseases and Chromium 6 in the city water and exhaust particles poisoning the homes around the airport. That's all they talk about. They keep threatening to move to the Rocky Mountains. I hope."

"So no blessing the children?" Jesus said.

"Think of the liability," Bishop Horkley said. "Anyway, these kids are so sensitive and easily startled, so scared of anything new. They'll scream *stranger danger* the minute you walk through the door."

"You don't think they'll recognize me?" Jesus said. He looked hurt.

"Well, maybe some of the older primary kids," the bishop said. "But even that's problematic. It's like Santa Claus. What kid doesn't love the idea of a fat man in a red suit dropping down the chimney with a sack full of gifts? But a fat man in a Santa suit at the Burbank Mall? Terrifying!"

"You think I'll scare them?" Jesus asked.

"The beard and the robe and the long hair," Bishop Horkley said. "Afraid so. I'm betting they think you're a homeless guy who just wandered in off the street. We've had a few of those."

"I really wanted to see the kids," Jesus said.

"Well, maybe we can do something," Bishop Horkley said. "I mean, you did travel a long way." He tapped his chin. "How about I go to the Primary room, tell the kids we have a special visitor, then I throw open the curtains, and you're outside the window, waving and blowing kisses. And then you kind of do this Mary Poppins-Harry Potter thing and float away."

"I don't know," Jesus said. "It sounds hokey."

"Nonsense," Bishop Horkley said. "Kids love that stuff. This is Southern California, Lord. You're competing with The Wizarding World of Harry Potter and Disneyland. Even better if you can shoot lasers from your eyes and hurl a couple of fireballs. That just might impress them."

Jesus scratched the back of his neck. "I'm kind of getting the feeling you don't need me."

Bishop Horkley let go a long breath, as if conceding something. He firmly gripped his chair's padded armrests. "Lord, apart from a couple of eccentrics in the ward, I'm running a tight ship here. You should see the members after sacrament meeting. They don't say a word, just quietly leave the chapel with bowed heads and folded arms. I've turned them into a God-fearing people.

You're a busy man, and I don't want to waste your time when the lost sheep are out *there*. But I really appreciate your visit." Bishop Horkley stood and moved toward the office door.

Jesus stood, too.

"Personally," Bishop Horkley said, leaning toward the Savior and speaking in a half whisper. "I think your time would be better spent in the Burbank 2nd Ward. You should see those heathens after sacrament meeting, shaking hands, embracing, talking, smiling. I've never seen such irreverence! And that new bishop with glasses. I've heard some ward members actually call him by his first name. Can you imagine that? The disrespect!"

"So there's nothing you need?" Jesus asked, shuffling through the door. "Nothing I can do?"

Bishop Horkley waved. "We're good. But it was great to finally meet you. Thanks for thinking of us, Lord. Really."

Bishop Horkley closed the door and stood there, his hand resting on the curved brass handle. Such a burning filled his breast, such peace and joy, that he could report personally to the Son of God that all was well in this small corner of Zion.

He took a step toward his desk, a lightness in his feet, as if he were levitating. Out of habit, he ran his hand over his hairless scalp but stopped and turned suddenly. What had Jesus asked before leaving? Was there something the bishop needed? Something the Savior could do? Of course! Bishop Horkley's hand shot out for the door handle. It had been twenty years since he'd savored the silken weight of a full head of hair. After all his years of dedication and service to the Kingdom, he deserved it!

Bishop Horkley threw the door open, panting in anticipation.

But the Savior was already gone.

Parley Young: One Mormon Life

Conception

"They're up there now," Bishop Gray croons from the pulpit. His eyes move to the chapel ceiling. "Trillions and Trillions of spirits waiting to inhabit mortal bodies, warriors saved for these perilous last days, ready to battle the Adversary in his strongest hour. And they need us, brothers and sisters, to bring them into this world."

The words crackle in Jackie's ears. A warmth fills her breast. Later that day, she tosses her birth control pills. Her husband John finds them under a limp lettuce leaf in the trash bin.

"What's the deal, Jackie?" he asks.

Shocked, she looks up from the cutting board where she slices carrots. "So many spirits up there," she says. "I don't want to be an old mother."

"But Jackie"—John's still holding the birth control pills—"you're only nineteen."

"Ten kids," she says. "That's what we talked about. Do you know how many years that takes? Think of our posterity. They're waiting for us."

Posterity. The word sends a thrilling ripple through John's groin.

Birth

4:30 a.m. Dark fluids seep from Jackie. Somewhere in the distance a garbage truck's hydraulic lift whines shrilly. Jackie mistakes the sound for the singing of angels.

John feels on the edge of consciousness. Again and again he swallows hard at a scalding acidity rising in the back of his throat. The delivery room tilts and then rights itself. He sees a fuzzy incandescence around the edges of things.

"A handsome baby boy," the doctor says, laying a white bundle on Jackie's breast.

"Parley," Jackie says. "That's what we'll name him."

Pale and nauseous, John is suddenly lucid. "You're joking, right? Isn't that your ancestor who fell in the . . ."

Jackie looks at him fiercely. "Back then it happened to a lot of people."

An Inspiring Name

They name Parley after his great-great-great-great grandfather, Parley Mordecai Young, a man who pulled a handcart across the snow-clogged plains in the winter of 1857, worked a sugar beet farm in southern Utah with his six wives, cranked out children into his seventies, and then expired one moonless night when he toppled down a well while searching for the privy.

Excerpt from Parley's Baby Blessing

John: *Parley, we bless you that you'll never wander dark paths and lose your way, that you'll never stumble into those abysses the Adversary has dug for the righteous, that your feet will always be planted on sweet gospel sod . . .*

Parley's Siblings

Nephi, Ezra, Emma, Eliza, Hyrum, Mary, Lucy, Heber, and Sidney.

A Family Vacation to San Francisco

Jaws slack, eyes protruding, passers-by stare as Parley and his siblings file out of their Ford Econoline van. A young woman with mangy dreadlocks and a peace sign tattooed on her left calf taps John on the shoulder. Her index finger stabs at the sky. "You're killing the earth," she screams.

Early Years

For his eighth birthday, Parley receives a small black tag inscribed with the words *Future Missionary*. He wears the tag to church, to school, to sleep, to the community swimming pool. He gives an illustrated Book of Mormon to a Baptist kid at school and invites him to Primary.

Favorite foods

Parley loves Jell-O, pot roast, black licorice, and tuna casserole.

First Date

Parley is sixteen. He irons his white shirt, fastidiously removes the lint from his suit jacket. The girl's name is Heather. Parley drives the family Econoline van. His parents, John and Jackie, sit quietly in the back of the van while Parley stands in a vaulted entryway and shakes hands with Heather's father, a portly bearded man, a sculptor and instructor at the state college who teaches a youth Sunday class at church.

"You like this painting?" Heather's father asks as Parley eyes the print hanging on the wall.

"She's not wearing any clothes," Parley says. "And she's standing in a giant clam."

"It's Boticelli's *Venus*," Heather's father says, staring at the woman's creamy thighs. "Gorgeous. Stunning."

Secretly, Parley disapproves.

Second Date

Cookies, punch, Parcheesi, Uno, the Ungame. Parley takes Heather home at 9:30 pm. That night he sleeps well and rises promptly at 6:30 am.

The Men's Room

After overindulging at a ward ice cream social, Parley experiences acute lactose intolerance.

Valedictorian, Penrose High School Graduation Ceremony

The first line of Parley's speech: *Infinity is not a number, but a direction. Similarly, our human potential . . .*

There's a sound like the chugging of a lawnmower fighting through thick grass, louder and louder. Parley pauses, looks up from the sheaf of papers on the podium and squints into the radiant sky. A small Cessna appears suddenly from the north and buzzes low over the crowded stadium. People gasp. They duck under their plastic chairs. The pilot, a man with a flat top and aviator shades, laughs hysterically in the cockpit, and his passenger, a blond woman, presses her ample breasts against the cabin window.

Superintendent Abbott shoves Parley aside. "Uhm. Yeah"—Abbot looks at the microphone as if it's something he's been asked to eat. A siren wails—"Folks. Yeah. Don't be alarmed. The Chief of Police feels we should evacuate the stadium. Exit in an orderly fashion, please."

Called to Serve

Parley's mission call, an excerpt: *You are assigned to labor in the Honduras San Pedro Sula Mission. You will prepare to preach the gospel in the Spanish language.*

Jackie pulls a map from the coat closet and spreads it across the dining room table. She's on the phone with Grandma Young.

"Yes, he just got his call," she yells into the phone. "Honduras. I see it right here on the map. It's in southern Mexico. Yes, I'm sure they have washing machines and microwaves there."

Parley dusts off his old junior high Spanish assignments. For dinner, Jackie makes tacos. John buys a piñata, which the family blithely pulverizes with a broomstick after dinner.

Farewell Talk at Church

Parley, excerpt from talk: *I echo the words of that great prophet Joseph Smith who, looking out over his beloved Nauvoo for the last time, said: "I go as a lamb to the slaughter; but I am calm as a summer's morning; I have a conscience void of sin and offense before God, and before all men. I shall die innocent, and it shall be said of me—he was murdered in cold blood."*

Parley weeps, Jackie weeps, John weeps, Grandma and Grandpa Young weep. Aunts, uncles, cousins, nephews, and nieces weep. Heather weeps, friends weep, babies weep. Priests and High Priests sleep. Bishop Sanders eyes his watch and nervously taps his Wingtips. A deacon brings up a fresh box of Kleenex.

Missionary Training Center: Provo, Utah

Savory Salisbury steak. Spaghetti in a rich meat sauce. Parley puts on weight. He devotes himself to learning Spanish. In fact, he never speaks a word of English.

Airport

Parley mutters goodbyes in Spanish. *"Adiós! Voy a convertir el mundo,"* he says. He embraces Jackie, embraces John, affectionately shakes Heather's hand. While he's away, Heather promises to plan their wedding.

First Night in Honduras

Fleas, ticks, chiggers, earwigs, gnats, roaches, rats. Bats, beetles, mice, mites, lice. Spitting spiders, jumping spiders, barking spiders, flying spiders. Fire ants, Azteca ants, Parasol ants, Tuxedo ants. Screaming monkeys. Diggers, gougers, itchers, stingers, stabbers. Iguanas. Mosquitoes.

Some Fatherly Advice

A letter from John, an excerpt: *Parley, an honorable mission is the foundation of a successful life. I truly believe that. Too many squander the experience. You might feel it's not in my character to say this, but let me impart some sage advice my father gave me before I left on my mission. "Son," he said, "keep your pecker in the bird house."*

Parley's First Baptism

Parley and Pedro Sanchez wade into the dark, meandering river. Piranhas nip at their heels, crocodiles dismember a yak corpse on the opposite bank, primitive savages beat drums in the distance.

Coming up from the water, Pedro embraces Parley and intones a lispy *Gracias* in his ear. Parley feels Pedro's hand clamped tightly around his right buttock. "What a strange custom," Parley thinks.

Altercation

A letter from Parley's companion, Elder Parker, to Guadalupe Rancho de la Lengua, an excerpt translated from Spanish: *What I wouldn't give to get some distance between me and this new elder. What's his name? Young? That's right. Every morning I have to wake up to his chipper voice and that stupid grin on his happy face. I want him to stop shining my shoes. I think I'll scream if he says even one more time with that dreamy look in his eyes, "Elder, these are our days in the history of the Church!" The only thing that makes life bearable is you, Guadalupe, seeing you across the chapel on Sundays, getting your letters. When I'm back in Utah, I'll send money for a plane ticket. We'll drive up Provo Canyon in my Mustang. We'll eat lunch in a grassy meadow above the tree line. You can make those cheese empanadas I love.*

Parley confronts Elder Parker about a romantic letter he finds on the bathroom sink. Parker denies everything. Parley also expresses concern over Elder Parker's lack of interest in their morning companionship study.

"You'll never understand our love," Parker says, and then, right before kicking Parley in the crotch, screams, "Put this in your journal!"

More Companion Problems

An excerpt from Parley's letter to his father John: *I just got transferred to a city off the Mosquito Coast called Trujillo. I'm now companions with Elder Ramirez. He's from Caracas and tells me he used to be a cage fighter, but gave it up when he joined the Church.*

I don't think he quite understands what we're supposed to do as missionaries. He's always trying to sell our investigators these Rolex knock-offs. He has a bunch of them looped around a string he's tied into the lining of his suit jacket, and at the end of a discussion, he opens his jacket and starts making his pitch. It's quite awkward. Do you think I should speak with Mission President Hurley?

One night Parley's suddenly awoken from a mildly erotic dream about Heather. They're in a city he doesn't recognize, sitting in the back of a taxi that speeds through empty streets. Inexplicably, they're both dressed in purple leisure suits. Heather delicately kneads the back of Parley's neck.

Awake, Parley hears naked feet moving over saltillo tile, a book falling, the swish of fabric. Through the pale darkness, Parley watches Ramirez thumbing through his wallet, pulling out crisp dollar bills, ogling Heather's senior picture.

"*Elder, Qué estás haciendo?*" Parley asks.

"*Amigo*," Ramirez hisses, and then in a broken, effeminate English, says, "the only thing in this world that gives orders is balls." His hair sticks up. His eyes are wild. "*Silenzio, Elder.*"

Dumped

Heather hasn't written in over a year. Parley assumes her heavy course load in Family Science at BYU must be the cause, and then one day a letter arrives. Instead of emanating the floral scent of Heather's Tommy Girl perfume, the letter reeks of dirty diapers.

Heather, excerpt from letter: *It just happened so quickly with Phil. I mean, it was just a group of us watching* The Never Ending Story, *and Phil and I were crying during all the same scenes, like in the end when Bastian and the Empress are sitting there and she has the last grain of sand from Fantasia in her palm. By that time, everyone got tired of the movie and left and it was just the two of us, and I was like, "This is my favorite movie ever," and he was like, "Yeah, mine too." It was like we were meant to be together. I mean, we love the same movie. It was a sign. Anyway, since I'd already planned our wedding, all I had to do was replace your name with Phil's on the invitations. It all just happened so quickly, the marriage and then the pregnancy. Crazy! I forgot to write. Forgive me. So have a good mission. There's someone out there for you. I'd write more, but I have to nurse Lizzy. She's been fussy lately. I think she has a rash.*

That night Parley quietly weeps into his pillow.

A Letter from Mission President Hurley

An excerpt: *Elder Young, next week I'm sending a new missionary your way, Elder Casper from Vernal, Utah, fresh from the Missionary Training Center. I'll expect you to train him well. Teach him to preach the gospel with boldness. Teach him Spanish. With increased responsibility come greater blessings.*

Looking over your last letter to me, I see you're contemplating a major in pre-law at BYU. As an attorney, I advise against it. As you see, I'm as big as a house. It came upon me suddenly in my early thirties. Too much sitting in courtrooms and conference rooms, too many lunches at Essex House and Jean Georges, all those billing hours to make partner. I let myself go. I can't even buy pants off the rack anymore. My knees are shot. If I could go back, I'd be a logger or a fisherman or a gentleman farmer. I'd learn how to cobble shoes. Law is death, Elder! Death and pain and loneliness. I'm a tender soul and they think I'm a monster. Find success and happiness serving the Lord, Elder Young. That's the secret.

A Trainer

They hike wooded hills, wade sewage-choked streams, knock on doors. They smile. They push pamphlets and copies of the Book of Mormon on the unbelieving. They pray for the poor and needy. They implore wayward members to return to church.

One day, a little boy stops them. He's digging in a trash heap. His fingers and cheeks are stained black, and he wears an enormous T-shirt with *Don't Piss Me Off, Butt-Munch* printed across the chest.

Conversation with boy translated from Spanish:

The boy points at Parley's black name tag. "That's my name, too."

"Your name?" Parley is confused. He feels he's missed something.

"Elder," the boy says. He smiles. His teeth are white and straight. His eyes are blue. "Elder's my first name."

Parley laughs and drops to one knee in front of the boy. "Elder. And where did you get a name like that?"

The boy stares at his grubby bare feet, suddenly shy. "My mommy said it was my daddy's first name, just like yours. You and my daddy have the same name. Do you know where he is? I never met him."

Elder Casper grins dumbly as he fumbles through a pocket-sized Spanish/English dictionary. "What's he saying? I caught about a third of it. His father. Is his father interested in hearing more about the Church?"

"Let's get out of here," Parley says.

Parley's Advice to Elder Casper

Don't drink the water, don't pet the dogs, don't ride horses, don't eat the dried fish, never share a bed with your companion, don't believe any girl who confesses her love for you, and keep your pecker in the birdhouse.

The Triumphant Return Home

Parley appears at the end of the jet way. His suit is in tatters. He has jock itch and an intestinal parasite. He has about him the smell of the jungle. The camera flashes blind him. He sprints through a paper banner that reads *Well done, good and faithful servant!* All weep.

Engagement

BYU. They both stand in the Taco Bell line. Parley orders a grilled stuffed burrito. She orders three soft tacos with extra cheese and a side order of pinto beans. Her name is Linda Slack. Three months later they marry.

Marriage

After admonishing Parley to never criticize his wife's donuts, the wizened temple sealer officiating the wedding ceremony declares, "I now pronounce you husband and wife for time and all eternity."

Parley leans over the altar, lips quivering, puckered, unsure. Contact.

Newlyweds

Parley and Linda live in a basement apartment off Center Street. At night, they hear the couple above them make raucous love.

On Wednesdays, the newlyweds take a pottery class together at the Orem Recreation Center. Parley feels something deeply spiritual as he kneads the soft clay. He's making a replica of Michelangelo's *David* for Linda's birthday.

"Mount Timpanogos?" the instructor asks, inspecting Parley's creation.

Parley delicately runs a scraper over the mound of clay. "No, Michelangelo's *David* in miniature. It's almost done."

The instructor leans forward. He peers at the clay over his spotted glasses. "Yes, *David*. Yes"—his mouth hangs open—"yes . . . a very abstract interpretation."

Two weeks later, Parley and Linda receive a form letter from the City of Orem's Parks and Recreation Department. An excerpt from the letter: *Dear Students, we regret to inform you that during the firing process, there was an unforeseen malfunction in the kiln's heating coils, causing an explosion that destroyed all the pottery. None of it was salvageable. We are deeply sorry. Please find the enclosed check for twenty dollars to cover this inconvenience. We hope to see you again, maybe this fall for our tole painting or quilting class.*

Pharmaceutical Sales Representative, Logan and W. Salt Lake City

Lipitor, Zithromax, Simvastatin, Ambien, Allegra. Parley sells them all. At church, he feels a strange discomfort each time the bishop casually asks if he has any free Viagra samples in his car.

First Home

Parley and Linda buy a home in Nibley, Utah. There's a willow tree in the front yard, a jungle gym out back, and a view of snow-capped mountains.

"A few kids, a dog," the real estate agent says, his voice echoing off the bare walls. "Plenty of room."

"Ten kids," Parley and Linda say at the same time.

The Birth of Scott Parley Young

Nausea, the bitter tang of bile, a growing belly, an alien life squirming beneath the stretched skin, perennial fatigue, a small cramp in the lower back, thirty-six hours of labor, an emergency C-section at 3:00 am.

"It's your uterus, Mrs. Young," Doctor York tells Linda the morning after the birth. He sighs deeply. "The uterus is damaged, too thin to endure another pregnancy. I wouldn't advise having another child."

Parley stands at the hospital window and looks down on a city park where a pee-wee football team runs drills. "An Isaac," Parley thinks, tapping the glass. "At least I'll have an Isaac."

Elders Quorum Chili Cook-off

Presidency meeting to plan the annual Nibley Third Ward Elders Quorum Chili Cook-off, an excerpt:

President Young: "I don't know about this flier for the chili cook-off. I don't know if I'm comfortable with it."

First counselor: "Is it the mariachi chili pepper, President Young? Is it his sombrero? Is it his curly, black mustache? Is it the big accordion the pepper's playing? Is it the *Ay caramba!* speech balloon above the pepper's head?"

President Young: "No, it's not that."

Second counselor: "Is it the flaming cauldron of chili next to the pepper? Is it the color of the flames, President? Are the flames too red?"

President Young: "It's not the chili or the flames. It's this veiled flatulence reference, this text under the pepper about how the evening's sure to end with a bang. Isn't it a little crass?"

Becoming Bishop Young

It is proposed that we sustain Parley Mordecai Young as bishop of the Nibley Third Ward. All in favor please manifest it by the raising of the right hand. Any opposed by the same sign.

Later that day:

"What is this?" Parley asks his first counselor, Chuck Pendleton.

"Well, Bishop, that's Sister Verken's grocery bill. The ward's been paying it for the last two years. She just can't eat that food from the bishop's storehouse. She's ninety years old."

"$300.00 at Natural Grocers?" Parley asks. "Two dozen free range eggs? Four pounds of 90% lean, grass-fed bison? Organic Jazz apples? Forty Nag Champa incense sticks?"

"Bishop, she says that storehouse food is too processed, too much sodium and fat and high-fructose corn syrup. And the salsa there is just way too spicy for her. That's what she tells me. And the incense is for her daily mindfulness meditation."

"What's wrong with Walmart and Winco?" Parley asks. "Or even better, La Rancherita Market? Have you seen their produce? Have you seen the size of their pineapples?"

33rd Birthday

A note from Scotty written in Parley's birthday card: *Here is your birthday card, daddy. Inside is a cupon for a hug. I glued a magnett on the back. Put it on the frige so you won't lose it. Use it when you need a hug. Luv you. Scotty.*

A Great Honor: The Sederberg Sales Award

Hank Tudor, Vice President of Sales for Seabrook Pharmaceuticals. An excerpt taken from his speech at the annual Seabrook sales meeting awards dinner in Indianapolis: *Though I can't say I know Parley that well, I have an immense respect for him. I haven't seen him much on the links or at night in the hospitability suite, but all of you know I remember about zilch when there's an open bar or a guy in a golf cart handing out free drinks (pause for laughter). Seriously, folks, it's an honor to award Parley the Sederberg Sales Award for our top sales rep.*

Anniversary Dinner at Fredrico's

"I wonder what this could be?" Linda asks, taking the large, gift-wrapped box from Parley and giving it a little shake. "Maybe that Pilates set I've talked about?"

"Pilates set?" Parley says. "This is a hundred times better. A thousand."

Giggling, Linda tears away the wrapping paper. Her laughter ceases. She stares at what's in her hands: a black metal box with a handle, four stainless steel plates attached to the top of the box, and a meat thermometer. "What is it?" she asks.

"A sun oven." Parley cuts a piece from his calzone and spears it with his fork. "You can cook a turkey in that thing. And trust me"—he leans forward, his voice a whisper—"when the economy fails and we're thrown back into the Stone Age, you won't need a Pilates set."

Trouble at Work

A letter to Parley from Sal Rose, Western Regional Senior Manager for Seabrook Pharmaceuticals, an excerpt: *Last Thursday I received a telephone call from your client, Doctor Gupta, closing his account with us. He explained that over the last few months he felt you were trying to foist your religion on him. He mentioned a number of pamphlets he'd received from you as well as visits whose purpose, he felt, had more to do with proselytizing your faith than business. While I value and respect your personal beliefs, your job at Seabrook is not a platform from which to preach. Please desist from doing so. Cordially, Sal Rose.*

Becoming Stake President Young

It's Saturday morning. The kitchen phone rings.

"Hello," Scotty says. "Hello. Hello."

The voice is low and breathy, practically unintelligible, broken by sobs and sniffles. "They want me to be stake president. Pray for me. Pray for me."

Scotty moves the phone to his other ear. "Who is this?" he asks.

Father-Son Time

"Now, Scotty, here was a fine figure of a man," Parley says, hefting a worn copy of Parley Mordecai Young's autobiography *Kicking Against the Pricks: A Life on the Range*. "My namesake, a man who could lift the backend of a wagon and walk fifty miles a day. And that's when he was in his seventies. He once wrestled a savage Indian for a pot of honey somewhere outside Omaha. Did you know that?"

"Didn't he have a bunch of wives?" Scotty asks.

"Well, those were different times," Parley says.

"Didn't he, like, have to go pee one night and fell into a well?" Scotty asks.

Parley shifts uneasily on the couch. "It was a dark night. Somebody moved the outhouse. Maybe it was a joke, one of the neighbor boys trying to get a cheap laugh." Parley sighs and stares out the living room window. He watches his neighbor, Rob Munson, apply a coat of wax to his new black Mercedes. "A shame, really," Parley says, setting his hand on Scotty's shoulder. "He could have lived another decade. Yes, that was when a man was a man, when you could see what you were made from by pitting yourself against the elements. Do you ever think about that, son," Parley asks, "pitting yourself against the elements?"

"I dunno," Scotty says, wiping his thumb under his nose and then onto his jeans.

Parley kneads Scotty's bicep. He's shocked at the loose flab there, at the gelatinous quiver under his fingertips. He looks at his son's round face. His skin is so pale, almost translucent. Parley has a sudden idea, a revelation. He rubs his palms together.

"What do you say, Scotty? This Saturday. Ten miles up to Box Elder Peak. Pit ourselves against the elements? We'll take some beef jerky."

"I dunno," Scotty says.

Concerns about America's Youth

Parley, an excerpt from his journal: *Kids these days! Waddling around with their guts hanging over their belts. All that fat and sugar. There's no self-control. They can't even do anything that requires a little discomfort. At the first tingle of pain they throw their arms up and quit. It's a pity we can't pull a handcart across the plains every ten years, pit ourselves against the steel-hard earth as a fierce blizzard pushes us backwards. That would be the life. That was when a man was a man.*

Stake President Young Chooses a Scout Camp

Pale Horse Survival Camp, an excerpt from its brochure: *No basket weaving at this scout camp, no cafeteria stocked with Fruity-Pebbles and crème brûlée. If your son wants to eat, he better sharpen a stick and get out in the woods. That's how we live here: off the fat of the land.*

Your son will spend the week living in primitive shelters. He'll feast on cattails, nettles, yard greens, acorns, and an assortment of wild game. He'll track cougars, hike to the top of Bald Mountain, and fashion clothing from animals he'll track and kill.

When the food shortages finally hit, when governments collapse, when formal education is worth nothing, this is what you'll want your son to have: the knowledge and confidence to survive. And that's what we'll give him.

A Bad Decision

An internal memo from Mark Bailey, legal counsel for The Church of Jesus Christ of Latter-day Saints, to Church leaders, an excerpt: *In August, we received a number of complaints from members of the Nibley Utah Stake, whose sons attended Pale Horse Survival Scout Camp outside Ketchum, Idaho, a camp chosen, they said, by Parley Young, president of the Stake. He felt that Camp Grizzly, the Stake's scout camp for the last five years, had become too lavish and costly, and missed the rugged spirit and survival focus of early scouting. After seeing Pale Horse's nominal fees, the scouts' parents agreed with President Young.*

When the scouts returned from Pale Horse at the end of July, parents claimed they couldn't recognize their sons. Many of the boys had lost a significant amount of weight. Their faces were painted black and most only wore fur loincloths made from either rabbit or possum. Additionally, all carried what looked like primitive weapons—spears and hatchets—fashioned from wood and stone.

In the weeks following, it seems most of the boys had difficulties readjusting to their old lives. One boy killed a neighbor's pet rabbit and ate it. Some prefer a shallow hole in the backyard over their beds. A few only speak in clipped phrases and grunts.

Their therapists, however, believe they're making wonderful progress and should return to school in January.

On multiple occasions, I attempted to contact the owner of this camp, a Sergeant Silko, but his staff tells me he's involved in some kind of U.S. government project in Islamabad, Pakistan. They're unsure when he'll return.

While President Young, whose son Scotty also attended the camp, never intentionally misled parents about the purpose of this survival camp, he does admit that he left out certain particulars, namely the tracking, hunting, and killing focus of the camp. Had they known this, most parents claim they would not have allowed their sons to attend. Further, many parents are also angry that their sons didn't bring home more merit badges.

Linda Changes the Locks

The front and back doors won't open. Parley's key doesn't fit the locks. He pushes at the door, pleads through the solid oak in a whisper, dials Linda's cell phone and stares up at the dark windows as the phone goes straight to voicemail. There's a white envelope under Linda's potted geraniums.

Excerpt from Linda's letter: *You're gone all the time trying to make your little heaven on earth, and you don't see that your own house is a den of dysfunction. Do you even know me anymore? Do you know your son? He didn't want to go to your stupid camp, but he went to make you happy. Now look at him. All he does is sit in the basement all day tying sticks together and beating that awful drum.*

You're so worried about the wicked world, always sounding the warning that if we don't watch and listen our lives will fall to pieces. Your family's falling apart, and you don't even see it.

Living in the Church: Day 1

Parley can't move into the Holiday Inn. There would be talk, rumors. He decides to stay in his office at the church.

There's the discomfort of the office's hard floor, the scratch of the carpet. Parley makes a bed of clothes he finds in the church lost and found. A child's faux-fur coat is tucked under his chin, and his feet are wrapped in a foul-smelling basketball jersey he'd mistakenly used as a pillow. Outside, a storm is brewing. Tree branches scrape across the windows. The building creaks and moans.

Living in the Church: Day 3

Parley buys a small air mattress from a sporting goods store. He bathes in the baptismal font and dries himself with a blue gingham tablecloth somebody left in the Relief Society room. He scours his shirt collars in the bathroom sink. In a strange way, this primitive living vaguely reminds him of his mission to Honduras, minus the malaria, monkeys, tropical rot, and intestinal parasites.

Long Nights

Parley lies there, teeth chattering, the night an endless discomfort as he thinks of Linda and Scotty. Who are their closest friends, what are their hobbies, their favorite books, their aspirations, hopes, and wishes? He doesn't know. What do they fear? Darkness, fog, wind, lightning? What do they fear most? Parley suddenly knows. The realization is like the shock of cold water. This loneliness and separation—that's what they fear most. Parley realizes that it's also what he fears most.

Caught

Sister Grover, returning to the church late one night to retrieve a piece of forgotten piano music, discovers Parley walking down the hallway, naked and slightly damp, wrapped in only a blue gingham tablecloth. She freezes, face as white as the cinderblock wall, her mouth a dark hole. She runs. Parley contemplates chasing her through the parking lot to explain things. Instead, he quickly retreats to his office.

Release

A letter of resignation from Parley to the First Presidency of the Church, an excerpt: *What does it profit a man if he lives only for other's praise, but not his family's? I went about the Lord's work with my ends in sight. I gave the least to those nearest me. I became a stranger to my family. I was desperate to be remembered by strangers and acquaintances. I lost perspective.*

A New Calling

Parley teaches a Sunday school class for the fourteen and fifteen year olds.

A questionnaire Parley gives his students on their first Sunday together, an excerpt:

1. *Name your two closest friends.*
2. *Name one of your hobbies.*
3. *What is your favorite music group?*
4. *What is your favorite sport?*
5. *What is your favorite song?*
6. *What are your aspirations, hopes, and dreams?*

Rhodophobia

Parley has a deep and inexplicable fear of the color red. Staring at the rich crimson of the raspberry jam Linda puts up every summer, he feels a sickening jolt in his lower stomach.

Dental Hygiene

Parley brushes three times a day and flosses regularly. He visits the dentist twice a year. His teeth are white and hard as granite.

A Secret Vice

Hidden in the pantry behind a fifty-pound sack of pinto beans, Parley keeps a case of diet Dr. Pepper. He can't help himself. He loves the taste.

Retirement

Genealogy consumes Parley. He traces his lineage back to Adam, disappointed he can go no further. He speaks proudly of Parley Mordecai Young's long journey across the plains, but is silent when Linda reminds him that he and Benedict Arnold are distantly related on his father's side.

Second Mission

Stricken, shrunken, half his former self, Parley starts and ends the day with a tall glass of frothy Metamucil. But still he accepts the call to work in the Stake Cannery. Because of the many complaints, he's prohibited from manning the jalapeno pepper station during salsa production.

Parley tries to explain to Linda the salutary benefits of spicy foods.

International Aid to Ghana

A letter from Parley to Edward Mufugavi, an excerpt: *Feed the Children sent me a picture of you. Truthfully, you're too skinny for an eight year old. But it's understandable. I've watched the Travel Channel's* Bizarre Foods. *I have a pretty good idea what dinner looks like in Ghana. In Honduras, I once ate a goat bladder stuffed with some kind of summer squash. It wasn't pleasant. Did I already tell you I lived in Honduras for two years? I know something about tropical afflictions.*

Hopefully the twenty dollars I send every month will reach your dinner plate. If not, let me know. I'll send it to you directly.

Chin up, Eddie. Hope you don't mind if I call you that? Life will get better. Soon the great Jehovah will declare His work done and usher in a thousand years of peace. It'll be paradise, plenty to eat, Eddie. No round worm and dysentery. Paradise awaits you, but don't count on it. Live life to the fullest. Hug your brother. Kiss your mother. Find your paradise now.

Golden Years

Parley can't remember the names of all his grandchildren and great-grandchildren. At family reunions he presides over the great congregation and smiles to himself, wondering how Abraham felt as he contemplated the sands of the sea.

Death

A floating sensation, the ringing of bells, a long tunnel of light leading upward. Parley moves through a billowing mist. A man in a white flowing robe greets him.

"Brother, follow me," the man says. "So much work to do, so little time."

"You look familiar," Parley says. "Did I know you?"

The man stops. "I forgot to introduce myself." He thrusts his hand forward. "We're related on your father's side. Arnold was my name, Benedict Arnold."

On the other side of town, Parley's eight-year-old great-grandson Baxter stands before a mirror, trying on a small black tag inscribed with the words *Future Missionary*.

Barry Dudson:
The God Journals

As man now is, God once was:
As God now is, man may be.

—Lorenzo Snow,
fifth President of The Church of
Jesus Christ of Latter-day Saints

And that same sociality which exists among us
here will exist among us there . . .

—Doctrine and Covenants 130:2

Yes! After 9 God years I have finally completed degree at Celestial Kingdom University. Very emotional as I sat in lustrous white robes with other CKU graduates under crystal chandeliers and gilded dome of Holy of Holies Auditorium, absorbing inspiring words of commencement speaker admonishing us to go forth and ascend our heavenly thrones, to create worlds and spirit offspring, to rule and reign in righteousness forever.

And after ceremony, still emotional as I held diploma, rereading elegant calligraphy declaring: *Celestial Kingdom University has conferred on Barry Dudson the rank of God and has granted this diploma as evidence thereof.* So emotional because road to godhood, for me, so long! Had to retake most of math and sciences classes. Had resolved in retirement to overcome lifelong math/science ineptitude by taking classes at local community college, but died of massive coronary in Burger King parking lot one year before retirement. Well, had to wait for post-earth life to reach goal, but finally did!

From this day forward, as official CKU graduate, have decided to keep detailed journal, a heavenly record, to document life as new god and soon-to-be proud father of many, many spirit children who will live on worlds I create. With journal, hope to provide anyone interested, maybe future generations, maybe soon-to-be gods and goddesses, a sense of my journey to godhood, and, as a god, all the decisions to make and matters to decide. Will call today God Day 1.

God Day 2

Hello, future generations! Forgot in last entry to mention super smart eternal companion Vivica, who, by the way, finished CKU degree with honors in 3 God years. Amazing! All through my ups and downs at CKU, Viv so surprisingly patient, so supportive as we lived in student housing, even as her parents, siblings, and friends moved on to occupy heavenly mansions in their everlasting kingdoms, while I retook classes.

Amazed at how different Viv and I are as gods, so unlike petty, mortal selves. Like as newlyweds in earth life, how Viv so critical when I forgot to drain dirty dishwater from sink or didn't form perfect "hospital corners" when making bed. And how I, sullen and resentful, would wait for her to run errands, then use her electric toothbrush to scrub skuzzy brown crust from around edges of kitchen sink. Now as partners in celestial journey, as god and goddess soon to create worlds and spirit offspring without end, so glad we've overcome mortal squabbles.

Now, as official CKU graduate, must wait for kingdom assignment. So excited to begin life as all-powerful god!!!

God Day 4

Well, have already missed one day of journal writing. Even gods sometimes forget things.

Thought I would share one delightful surprise of godhood: perfected body! Chiseled biceps, washboard abs, thick mane of blond hair. In life, was very large bald man, what doctors called obese. Strange to look down now and see feet and genitals.

Will admit: was compulsive overeater in earth life. Wasn't just big bones and faulty thyroid that parents and grandparents, also enormous, blamed. Long history of

Dudson family struggle with weight going back to great-great-great grandfather Erastus "Pork Chop" Dudson, first member of Mormon church in family who famously stopped walking one mile after beginning journey to Utah, then waited thirteen years for Central Pacific to build rail line with first-class dining car to Salt Lake City. All those generations! How many Dudsons were chubbiest kid at school? How many teased to no end about fleshy jowls and saggy breasts?

As a child, was so depressed about flabby body. Coped by eating through boxes of HoHos and Little Debbie Nutty Buddy Bars secretly purchased with birthday money and hidden in bedroom closet. By high school, wore special spandex undershirts to contain jiggly breasts and protruding belly. As young adult just out of college and living alone, once bought large dog muzzle from local pet store to wear around studio apartment in desperate and absurd attempt to stop snacking. Had such a warped view of food, like thinking everything at Trader Joe's was healthy, then feeling justified scarfing down three boxes of chocolate almond butter tarts because package said portion of profits would go to restore 200,000 acres of rainforest.

And then by mid fifties, knees and back shot, blood pressure through roof. Could only fit slacks and shirts custom ordered from Handsome and Hefty, company out of Tulsa, Oklahoma that also made tents and tarps. Deluded self with lifetime of justifications not to lose weight. So many excuses! And then dying of massive coronary in Burger King parking lot, a smear of barbeque sauce still on chin.

Hated mortal self. So happy to be done with bloated, unwieldy body.

God Day 5

Just read over previous entry. Such a downer! Must apologize. Don't want to be dark cloud because now, as buff, all-powerful god, with awesome goddess wife, everything so great!

Will share something positive, another delightful surprise of godhood: Viv's sexy, perfected body. Grrrrrrrrr! Curvy and buxom, skin like ivory. Can't stop ogling her. And she's just as surprised by perfected body: always standing in front of mirror, staring at self with disbelief, caressing taut, flawless thighs once pocked with cellulite and bursts of purple veins. Even crooked nose from college cooking accident involving cast iron frying pan now perfect.

But enough sexy thoughts about Viv. So much work to do. Spirits to create! Matter to organize!

God Day 6

Exciting day! Received kingdom assignment from Department of Celestial Housing and Galactic Development (DCHGD). Viv and I now proud owners of galaxy MACS0647-JD, really nice piece of space with some breathtaking star cluster and spiral galaxy views, and—

because universe always expanding—plenty of room to fill with worlds for spirit children.

God Day 13

Oops, has been a while since last entry. Very good excuse, though. Spent very productive week creating spirit offspring with Viv.

In mortal life, could never quite picture heavenly parents creating spirits. Never really discussed in Sunday school. As teenager, imagined (and hoped) for steamy lovemaking on bed of billowing clouds with heavenly wife who might vaguely resemble actress Scarlett Johansson. Somewhat disappointed by spirit-creation process. Really more of Viv and I telepathically collecting star dust by raising hands to heavens and intoning sacred words with commanding, godly voices. No steamy lovemaking atop clouds required.

But then so awesome to see spirit children grow! Process like watching tadpoles mature, first foot and then arm, and then another foot and arm, and soon crawling, taking first steps, falling, speaking gibberish.

Good to see smile on Viv's perfect face—so happy, so content as heavenly mother to many, many spirits. Can't help just putting arm around her and soaking up pure joy of watching spirit children grow.

God Day 14

Have confession, future generations: am really nervous about being first-time father. Was never father on earth because mortal body couldn't produce essential protein for viable sperm. Planned to adopt children, but spent ten years on waiting list before giving up. Adoption agency finally said teenage moms probably not interested in plus-size couples.

In first years of marriage, broke heart to find Viv's Internet search histories for baby clothes, the long stares at toddling children at McDonald's, the crying in locked bathroom with shower running.

But all painful memories of infertility now gone as I watch spirit children—my children—maturing, asking questions about earth life. How to respond? How to prepare them for life's harsh realities? Beginning to wonder if earthly suffering really necessary? Don't parents want a better life for children, better than life they had? Nothing wrong with that, right?

Well, no time to write more. Must think about mortal bodies for spirit children.

God Day 15

After much thought, have decided not to burden children with obesity. Obesity will not exist in world Viv and I create!

In fact, have decided to do away with all sickness, disease, handicaps, delays, and deformities. None! Will make all children beautiful, athletic specimens. Will test and try them instead with trappings of beauty: vanity, pride, narcissism, shallowness, etc. No bad breath, jock itch, hemorrhoids, flatulence, diarrhea, profuse sweating. All embarrassing maladies of earth life gone! Never will they experience gastrointestinal assault from eating pound of old cold cuts, speeding home at eighty miles an hour, then pulling off road to explosively relieve self in stranger's side yard while passing mail carrier pretends not to notice fat man squatting in bushes. In fact, no defecation or urination! Will create biological process by which waste leaves body through skin pores as aromatic vapor smelling like freshly baked cinnamon rolls.

Viv really excited about modifications. "But what about female complaints?" she asked, rocking armload of spirit children. "Bleeding an entire week every month! How's that fair?" Totally agree. So, as per Viv's recommendations: no vaginal birth, no menstruation, no sitdown peeing, no fuzzy upper lips and chins, no hairy legs, and upper body strength equal to men's.

This I declare!

God Day 16

Lately, can't let go of one nagging thought. Is this: how is God not crushed by sadness of omniscience? Like staring into a child's eyes and seeing chain of poor decisions that will lead to unhappiness and eventual damnation.

Couldn't help thinking about this all day with great sadness, but, after much pondering, have come to conclusion: As god, will switch off omniscient powers. Can't bear to see which of spirit children will not return to heavenly home. Absolutely crushing. Can't do it!

God Day 17

Spirit children maturing so quickly! Almost ready for mortal existence. Time to create earth.

Said to Viv with deep, authoritative voice while gazing down at space's great formless void: "Shall we go down to organize and form the heavens and the earth?" Wouldn't think of creating world without her. But Viv just looked up from gaggle of spirit children at feet and said with sad voice that knows this moment with spirit children won't last forever: "Barry, you go. I want a little more time with them." Had to turn away to hide great godly tears. Want endless happiness for Viv. Want her to look down on smiling children. If children are happy, then Viv is happy. Have sudden thought: why not just give children beautiful earth, beautiful sun-filled days with soft breezes, sandy beaches, and swaying palm trees? Don't parents want the best for their children?

God Day 43

Wow, creation not easy. Very complicated. Kept having to reference class notes from CKU. Handwriting so bad! Barely legible! But am proud that after 26 days of dividing light from darkness, water from dry land, planting grass, herbs, fruit trees, making all fish in sea, fowl in air, every creeping thing that creepeth upon the face of the earth, have finished.

Made some minor modifications during creation process. Well, maybe major modifications—like tweaking earth's axis so sun always plentiful.

Also, got a little carried away creating flowers, but kind of figured: "I'm God. I can do what I want." Have always loved flowers since taking floral arrangement class in high school. Always thought: how cool if all flowers glowed, like actually emitting light. Imagined myself at night, skipping through fields of glowing tulips and carnations. Never told fantasy to anyone. Actually a little embarrassing now that I think about it. So, as all-powerful god, have made modifications to chemical composition of all flowers, infusing petals with powerful element called Virilium, undiscovered on earth, to give them bright indigo glow at night.

Hard to believe that I, Barry Dudson, very large man on earth who struggled even clipping toenails and replacing windshield wiper blades, has created an earth.

Can't wait for children to see and experience grand world!

God Day 44

Now must consider medium to express message of salvation so children find spiritual path back to heavenly home.

In life, was great lover of music. Sang in high school jazz choir. Was backing vocalist for local doo-wop band of very large men called The Chubby Checkers. Very popular at weddings, retirement parties, convalescent homes, and one bar mitzvah.

All this to say that I've decided to make music the medium through which to speak to mortal children.

Prophets proclaiming message of salvation won't be skinny, bearded men wandering in from desert, but virtuoso crooners in mock turtlenecks and red sharkskin suits, belting out catchy words of salvation to adoring crowds—Frank Sinatra and Tony Bennett in their primes. And Savior of world, Christ figure to save all humanity? Will be greatest singer to ever live! Will be Singing Savior!

God Day 45

Have decided that first-born spirit child, Chip, will be Singing Savior. Not brightest of spirit children, but very sweet, very sensitive. Took Chip aside to extend great honor.

Said: "Well, Chip, as my firstborn I'd like you to be the Singing Savior, king of kings, and lord of lords, declaring in song the gospel of salvation to all my children. The prophets will sing of you. Many will look for the day of your birth."

This kind of piqued Chip's interest.

"A king?" Chip said. "Like, I get a sword and a golden throne?"

Chunked little guy in upper arm. Thought: So cute, so innocent.

Said: "Son, I'm loving your excitement, but no sword, no golden throne. In fact, you'll be a pacifist, born in lowly circumstances. Most will despise your simple message of love, but you'll have a few loyal followers—though most of them will turn on you. Oh, and those who despise you: there's a really good chance they'll eventually kill you in the most prolonged and painful way ever invented. And I forgot: before you're tortured to death, you need to take upon yourself the sins of all who've lived and will live, even those who'll kill you, and you'll sweat great drops of blood and writhe in agony."

Wow, kind of didn't realize awfulness of job until I actually had to describe it. Maybe was too blunt. As first-time father, still learning how to effectively speak with children. Probably didn't explain whole Singing Savior thing that well.

Said: "Son, what do you think? You up for it? What an honor, right?"

Chip kind of looked up at me, not saying anything, then cried for two hours.

God Day 46

With Chip unwilling to be Singing Savior, and really not even speaking to me anymore, have offered holy calling to next spirit child, Addison. Not interested. And then to next, Bobbie. And then to Dylan, Harper, Jordan, Pat, Reese, and Taylor. All declined. Just asked 3,289th child, Tim. Again, declined.

Maybe word got around about difficult role of Singing Savior. Now, all children avoiding me, always too busy when I come around, always rushing off to some place. "Sorry, Dad, no time to talk," they say.

Freaking out just a little. Must have Savior figure to lead children back to heavenly home, to atone for sins.

Will stay calm and table problem. Still have few thousand human years to find Singing Savior.

God Day 47

Okay, future generations, big day has arrived! Time to send spirit children down to beautiful earth I created, to try and test them, to refine them in the great crucible of mortality, all in the hope they'll return to us and eventually ascend to their own heavenly thrones.

Viv an emotional mess: bottom lip trembling, tears soaking her heavenly robes. Well, must admit that I'm barely keeping it together myself. Like good father, hoping for the best. Hoping spirit children follow strait and narrow path, and return to heavenly home.

God Day 48

Future generations, how to describe godly joy of watching children grow and mature?

Only a hundred earth years in and everything going so well, way better than expected, way better than crappy earth life I remember, with the political turmoil, wars, diseases, poverty, and famines playing out every night in gory detail on the evening news.

Amazed that nothing like that exists among children! In fact, quite the opposite: It's like children are living in a state of heightened civilization, no war and greed, just an equitable social order promoting cultural creation! No chaos and insecurity to stifle their indomitable will to learn and understand their marvelous world. They spend blissful days in pursuit of science and art, serving one another with kindness, welcoming singing prophets and embracing their catchy message of love. Can't help patting self on back—in very humble, god-like way—for creating such bounteous, temperate earth where all is beautiful, with plenty to eat and drink.

Have to remember to keep ego in check when listening to children's prayers: "Dear God, thank you for the glowing flowers"; "Dear God, thank you for the singing prophets and their toe-tapping message;" "Dear God, thank you for the soft breezes and the plentiful sunshine."

So much enjoyment now in gazing down at productive children. And then to hold spirit children awaiting bodies and say, "Look at it down there, all your brothers and sisters living in peace and harmony. Soon you'll be down there, too."

All wonderful until Viv, arms and lap brimming with spirit children, says with slightly perplexed look on perfect face, "Strange that none of our children have come home. I mean, I know it's not a pleasant thought, Barry, but people die. They get sick, they have accidents, they grow old."

Feel my jaw drop open. Have been so caught up with earth children's accomplishments, that haven't considered this. Quickly allay Viv's concerns by touting earth's pure air and clean water, the pesticide free cornucopia of fruits and vegetables and grains, the prosperous social order. And what does it all mean? I tell her: High life expectancy, outrageously high life expectancy, biblical life expectancy! Say this knowing something doesn't feel quite right. Say this knowing I might have made huge mistake!

God Day 49

Yes, on closer look at earth children, now see that I've made huge mistake! Problem is this: Earth children, with superior intellect, have developed very complicated process to extract Virilium from glowing flowers, and have used this Virilium to create powerful serum administered to fetus in utero that eliminates cellular degeneration and mutation. Even repairs damaged cells. No more heart disease. No more cancer. Not even the common cold! And accidents? Traumatic brain injury, cracked skull, compound fractures? Not an issue. One shot of Virilium and ten minutes later, not a scratch. Almost can't believe it: children have eliminated death! I mean, as earth father, would have been so proud, would have clapped hands and wept as children received Nobel Prize, but death kind of big deal, kind of essential for eternal progression. What does this mean? The reality is mind-blowing—even for a god: no spirits returning to loving arms of heavenly parents, no final judgment highlighting and touting children's earthly accomplishments, no resurrection, no warm embrace as I say, "Well done, sweet child, welcome to godhood." Can't bring myself to tell Viv. Can't bear to see fisted hand on hip and cutting stink-eye (posture Viv often used in earth life and now, as goddess, a posture she's perfected). What to do? Don't know. Will wait until absolutely essential to tell Viv—approach I often took in earth life.

God Day 50

Continue to tout to Viv pristine, unpolluted, nonviolent world as reason for children's freakish longevity. Randomly, have begun to reference long-lived prophets of bible to allay her concerns. For example, might clap hands in joyful display and say, "Viv, we got a bunch of Methuselahs down there!" Say this while experiencing a terrible guilt.

Children living to be 1,000+ years old! Not normal! And with deathless world, know that population will soon increase until all livable space gone. Soon, whole debacle of deathless world will really be obvious to Viv!

And in all this, just have to keep sending spirit children down to inhabit available bodies.

God Day 51

Quite obvious now that beautiful world is filling up with children.

Went to very edge of universe and sat atop magnificent, star-embedded nebula to contemplate predicament. Thought of pirate card game Viv and I used to play with earth friends. Whole point was to destroy other players with scurvy, explosive dysentery, typhoons, and ravenous cannibals.

Gosh, feel so bad hoping for catastrophic event to decimate earth children.

God Day 55

Today, after more than 3,000 earth years with no children returning to heavenly home, have finally confessed to Viv that children will never return, that children, in fact, will forever live an eternal mortal existence. Had to tell her since earth children, having filled world, stopped having children. Are now content just to enjoy healthy life on beautiful planet. No bodies to send spirits to. And with no reproduction, whole process of eternal progression grinds to a halt. Spirit children just hanging out, bored, nagging us about their turn on earth.

After explaining all to Viv, the Virilium and the serum, tried to soften poor decision by articulating good intentions of giving children a beautiful world and lives way better than ours. Viv threw me scalding stink-eye, done with perfection. But luckily Viv, as perfected, celestial being, no longer throwing cookware and hair brushes.

"Good intentions?" Viv said. "I assumed you'd learned something about good intentions on earth."

Ouch! Low blow but deserved. A reference to major financial mistake in earth life, all done with very good intentions because man at church, perhaps not very honest, convinced me to sink most of retirement into a herd of alpacas. He said alpaca sweaters would be next fashion craze. Invested with grand vision of Viv and me traveling world in oversize first-class seating, motoring through St. Peter's Basilica and Piccadilly Circus in custom-made Jazzy scooters. Never got clear answer about what happened to alpacas, but did hear that their teeth fell out before they died.

Could see disappointment on Viv's beautiful, perfected face, that familiar expression from our earth life, as if she were saying, "Way to go, Barry. How you gonna fix this mess?"

God Day 56

Spent most of day in dark funk, staring down at earth.

Keep mulling over one option: Could give distant meteor a little nudge. Could shake sun just enough so solar eruption burns earth to charcoal crisp. Kind of ungodly thought. How could a father, without provocation, destroy his sweet children?

But earlier did consult *The Code of Gods and Goddesses, Volume 1* just to make sure, and, yes, destroying children not a good idea. Article 3 states: "*In cases of general wickedness and unrighteousness, plagues, including but not limited to blood-tinged water, deafening frogs, fiery hail, lice, and locusts, may be used to rectify behavior. Only in cases of universal wickedness and unrighteousness, after god or goddess has repeatedly attempted to rectify errant children, is the use of global destruction warranted.*"

Gazing down, what do I see? Paradise, a utopia, no rich or poor, no hunger or disease. No errant children.

God Day 58

Funk continues. Can't bear to look down at earth children. Spent last couple days in bed, then this morning, surprised to receive Inter-Celestial Communiqué from Brother Birch, god of neighboring galaxy. It said:

Dear Brother Dudson,

I hope this communiqué finds you well.

This is a slightly awkward matter to broach, but yesterday I discovered that a number of your children are occupying a planet I'd already prepped for my own children. With millions of light years separating our galaxies, you can imagine my shock at finding them there, especially since I've never heard of mortals leaving their galaxy for another. I can only assume you placed them there—perhaps just an honest error.

I can see they're a good bunch of kids, happy and hardworking, quite industrious, not those lazy, degenerate types Father cleansed with the flood. I'm sure you're proud.

Let me know how to proceed.

Your celestial brother,
Brother Birch

I couldn't believe it! Quickly beamed down to earth. Not a soul, no one, completely empty! Not even a straggler or two. Can't understand what happened. How could children leave earth and travel across vast distances of space? Beamed to global research centers and laboratories children had created. Found plans and brilliant schematics for intricate rocket ships, fueled by Virilium, with ability to propel a spacecraft to light speed. In space observatories found star maps of wormhole networks gods use to travel through universe.

So proud! So sad! How should I feel, future generations? How? How?

God Day 59

Have screwed up this whole godhood thing. Wanted to do things differently. Wanted to bring more happiness into dark universe. Wanted to make *God* synonymous with all things wonderful. Wanted God to be present for all, not just some distant authority figure.

Will admit that during time on earth, God scared me with His great silence. Always felt His silence around me as I lay in bed at night, the day's stinging humiliation circuiting through my mind. Thought of God as enormous spider staring down at me from web littered with the dry husks of dead insects. Silent. Distant. Scary. Obeyed Him my whole life, maybe out of fear.

Was still resentful, even after death—maybe more resentful. With death, could see my whole mortal life, every moment from time as blot of goo in mother's uterus to last crushing beat of my heart in Burger King parking lot. And all the tragic in-between: a fat child with his hand in a peanut butter jar, a fat teenager eating a stick of butter, a fat adult stuck in an elevator. So much humiliation, so many moments of weakness, so much self-abuse. A lifetime of it. But tried every day to stay positive, tried to put one foot in front of the other while lumbering through gauntlet of taunts and oinks and atomic wedgies. Who wouldn't feel bad for that self-loathing fat man?

On earth, always prayed, always asked the deep questions that bothered me. Would ask, "God, why are you so mean? All those people who died in the flood. Even the children. The slaughter of the Canaanites, the execution of those poor Israelites for just looking at a golden calf. Why? Did it really happen? Was it just creative license? A bunch of bored medieval monks craving some adventure? Please tell me it was just that. And me? Why are you silent when I cry out at night, when I want you to take away the hurt and the embarrassment? Why don't you stop it?" But never an answer.

While at CKU, finally did send God a letter telling Him everything. Have never told Viv this. Hoped God would finally reveal the secret of human suffering, and why His great silence.

His response: "Dear Barry, I appreciate your letter. I know this won't satisfy you, but I can't answer your questions. The Universe won't let me. I know you're angry. I know you felt alone. All I can say is that the journey continues, far beyond here, and someday you'll find the answers. With affection and understanding, God."

And I didn't understand, not at CKU, not as Viv and I created spirit children, not as I summoned a world into existence. Through all that, held tightly to that kernel of resentment for God, always thinking: "I'll be the cool

God, the hugging God, the shoulder-to-cry-on God, the lean-on-me God."

And now, staring down at an empty earth, maybe I understand a little more. Maybe the cool God, the hugging God, just ends up as the God of a deserted world.

God Day 60

This afternoon, went looking for Chip, firstborn child. Finally, found him hiding behind the couch.

"Listen here, Chip," I said. "You're gonna be the Singing Savior." And then came the tears and the thumb sucking and the pleading. "Yes, it will be uncomfortable," I said, "and painful and lonely. People will despise you and spit on you and call you the worse names imaginable. But you'll keep at it, despite all the rottenness around you, until you make the greatest sacrifice anyone can make. You can do it, Chip. I know you can."

Had a second part to the speech, comforting words, affirming words, words to inspire and uplift, but there was no need. Suddenly, the tears and the wailing stopped. Chip stood up, a fierce glint in his eyes. He wiped at his dripping nose and said, "Okay, dad. I'll do it."

So proud!

God Day 61

This morning, with Viv at my side, gathered spirit children for very serious talk.

Said: "Dearest children, tomorrow your mother and I will go down to create a new world, a world that will be subject to decay and disorder. In fact, order and peace will be the exception. And what will determine your standing in that world? For the most part, nothing more than a genetic toss of the dice.

Most of you will live average lives: average looks, average grades, average jobs that will pay just enough for you to get away a couple weeks a year. You'll pass your lives in bland suburban homes with a couple of kids, and then you'll grow old and die, and it will be said at your funeral that you lived a good life, and then you'll be forgotten.

Some of you, a lucky few, will emerge into the world at the top of the socioeconomic ladder, with facial symmetry like the gods, sculpted cheekbones and full, pouty lips. And when you glide into a room, people will turn and stare, and when you speak, they'll hang on your every word. You'll be persuasive and elegant, instantly likeable and trustworthy. History will remember you as stalwarts of business, politics, and medicine, forever honored and studied.

And now you, my fat children, my unattractive children—yes, my favorites. How you'll suffer through life, with pants that never quite fit right, with damp armpits, with lungs constantly gasping for breath. You will pass through a gauntlet of hateful stares and daily put-downs, openly and privately ridiculed, an easy target for bullies. But don't despair, my fat children. From the shadowed corners where you'll seek shelter from life's ridicule, I want you to look up at the night sky where I'll place a constellation for you: an enormous man and woman whose faces say it all, a million endured offenses, a life with little affection, both in the tight embrace of a loving god as fat as they are, who bends to them and whispers: 'My beloved plus-size children, I know perfectly what you endure, for I have endured it, too.'"

With my words still ringing in the ether, I closed my eyes and remembered my earthly body, the great amorphous bulk of it, the unwieldy gravitational tug on all that flesh. From deep within, I summoned godly powers of physical transformation. Could feel perfect, sculpted body morph into doughy mass: cheeks sagging, jiggle of fleshy pouch under chin, droopy tickle of hairy belly against upper thighs, fingers swelling into pink sausages.

Opened eyes and gazed at Viv, who smiled at me with perfect understanding, cheeks wet with tears. I marveled at her transformation, at her rotund cheeks, the crooked nose I remembered from earth, the swell of her colossal breasts straining the white linen of her heavenly robe, and the broad shelf of her backside. How I'd missed all of it!

Smiling back at Viv, I flipped on my omniscient powers. Could instantly see arc of our lives stretching forever into eternities. Then looked out at vast multitude of spirit children and saw perfectly a trillion trajectories, some returning to Viv and me, and others never to return. But could feel it in deepest part of godly heart, the most profound love for them. For each of them. Understood, perhaps for first time, the beauty of all things, perfect and imperfect.

RYAN SHOEMAKER's debut story collection, *Beyond the Lights*, is available through No Record Press. T.C. Boyle called it a collection that "moves effortlessly from brilliant comedic pieces to stories of deep emotional resonance." Ryan's short fiction has appeared in *Gulf Stream, Santa Monica Review, Booth,* and *New Ohio Review,* among others.

www.ingramcontent.com/pod-product-compliance
Lightning Source LLC
Chambersburg PA
CBHW051507050726
47594CB00010B/4002